ON THE
SKY'S
CLAYEY BOTTOM:
SKETCHES
AND
HAPPENINGS
FROM THE
YEARS OF SILENCE

Zdeněk Urbánek
ON THE SKY'S CLAYEY BOTTOM

Sketches and Happenings from the Years of Silence

Translated by William Harkins

Four Walls Eight Windows
NEW YORK • LONDON

A Four Walls Eight Windows First Edition

Copyright ©1992 Zdeněk Urbánek
Introduction copyright ©1992 Václav Havel

First Printing May 1992
All Rights Reserved

Library of Congress Cataloging-in-Publication Data
Urbánek, Zdeněk
On the sky's clayey bottom:
sketches and happenings from the years of silence /
Zdeněk Urbánek; translated [from the Czech] by William Harkins
p.   cm.
ISBN 0-941423-76-X: $17.95
I. Title.
PG5038.U744A26   1992
891.8'635—dc20   91-39511
                                                                  CIP

Four Walls Eight Windows
P.O. Box 548
Village Station
New York, NY 10014

Jacket and interior Design by Martin Moskof
Printed in the U.S.A.

TABLE OF
CONTENTS

INTRODUCTION

When I was about twenty years of age and was trying to form an acquaintance with Czech theater and literature, I met Zdeněk Urbánek. I respected him as a writer of short stories and essays and as a translator, but at that time he scarcely belonged to those who captivated my interest most keenly. Only some fifteen years later, when intellectual opposition sharpened to our totalitarian regime and I was shut up in prison, did I discover quite by chance an earlier novel of Zdeněk's called *The Road to Don Quixote*, a story loosely based on Cervantes's young years in an Algerian prison. I was struck by the prophetically modern quality of the work and the imaginative sense captured by a writer of fiction of what it really feels like to be a prisoner. Since then I have followed my friend and my assistant (in the activities of the Charter 77 group) more closely. Without him I can hardly form an adequate conception of what Czech fiction, Czech essay writing, or Czech translation today have to tell us.

—Václav Havel

The Visit

"Wait, wait a minute," he said, out of breath. He had run up the four flights and caught me at the door. I had just banged it behind me. I was on my way to the post office with a parcel for my parents. He was wearing a translucent green-gray plastic raincoat and was wiping his face with his handkerchief.

"Is your wife at home?"

"No, she left town for the holidays."

"So wait, please, let's go back in. I'm Hruška from State Security," and he pushed some sort of card in a transparent case under my nose. "Your wife's away on vacation—that's too bad."

We went back inside and he kept on wiping his face. The plastic raincoat rustled when he took it off.

"It's kind of humid—there'll be a storm," he said, and sat down. "So you'll have to do for the two of you, since your wife isn't home."

He pulled a paper out of his pocket and was reading it.

"Do you know the Honces? They live downstairs."

1

"Yes, I know them. He's a tailor, a very fine person. He likes to go fishing."

"That doesn't matter. They're going to have a guest. You know, all sorts of visitors are coming for the Spartacade and we have to know what they're up to here. It's too bad your wife isn't home. We're told she's very good at that. But you can do just as well, can't you?"

"I don't know exactly what you want. Mr. Honc is a very fine man, he sometimes mends our clothes and recently he made a coat for our daughter, so I know him. His wife works somewhere too. They have a little girl. It's a very fine family."

"OK, but a stranger's going to stay with them and you surely understand what I'm trying to say. Whom they meet, who comes to see them, what their views are, what the visitors tell them, and where they take them. We have to be certain. For some they're beloved guests, for us they're a lot of work—just so we understand each other. Your wife was recommended to us, but since you have a wife who's so reliable, you too might be up to it. So what do you say? Whenever you sense anything that's not in order, come in and report it right away. We have to make certain. People say beloved guests, but it's sure a lot of work for us. So what do you say, can we count on you?"

"The Honces are very good people, that I'll guarantee."

"All right, but we've got to know what their visitor

is up to here, and they aren't Party members. Are you a member, Comrade?"

"No."

"But your wife is, I've got it here in black and white."

"No."

He scrutinized the paper for a while and suddenly got up.

"It's a mistake then. Is her name Milada Urbanová?"

"No. Urbanová lives two flights down."

The plastic raincoat rustled again as he threw it over his arm with a jerk.

"If we should find out that you've told anyone about my visit or the fact that they're being watched, you can count on having unpleasant consequences for yourself."

"I know that."

"We have to be sure. But why they told me downstairs that the apartment was on the fourth floor, I'll never understand. People always seem to have something against us. So remember—if we hear anything . . ."

"I understand."

"We're already loaded down with work and they send me another two floors up. Goodbye then. And keep quiet or you'll get it."

The Figure Swimmer

The last day of the year. Whatever has been passed over in the course of the year must be rushed through. But it is no use. The janitor's wife comes through with notice of the new rent, the postman comes and wants to chat before he takes away his reward for service rendered, and then there comes a visitor who is totally unexpected. A man nearly fifty, but with a face wonderfully smooth and fresh, although he does limp a little bit and supports himself on a cane, although . . .

"I wouldn't want anyone to find out about it, I beg you, don't tell anyone, even by chance, my wife, my daughter—them especially. It came to me—I happen to sleep poorly at night: I go over things, I try to find things I could do, I don't like to give in to it—and so I thought about you, your working in films, you know. Maybe you've heard about it. I had a stroke about a year ago, it took my whole side and my head as well. I recovered; but you know, I don't feel like going back to the drugstore. It would remind me of my illness, and of all those illnesses that the people have who come in there. And then the way things are going on in those drugstores nowadays. I'd be ashamed—the way they handle deliveries now—it's really terrible the way they do it today. But I did have a model drugstore—you may know it—in Jinonice. All the inhabitants of Waltrovka came there. I knew all the factory representatives and had friends among the doctors. They'd have assigned me to another drugstore right away, they promised me that: I could have managed it for them. But as it's done today, it goes against my grain—I would like to spend my time in the open air. So at nights I thought it over and I thought of you, since you're in films and you're well known. I do know Jiří Srnka. Once I happened to spend New Year's Eve with him—the party was really in fine spirits. I knew Eman Fiala too, but I knew his brother Ferenc Futurista better—he came to our drugstore. My former boss had a wonderful drugstore, the finest, maybe, in Prague, in size maybe the biggest after Adam's. Then I hadn't met with him as yet. I was following after him and he took hold of me and said, 'Jindříšek, if we only live to see it, I'll set up a drugstore such as the Republic has never seen.' He traveled a great deal, he knew America, England, all of it. And he wanted to set up a drugstore like one he had seen in Basel. He was always talking about it. He forgave me even though at one time he probably didn't even want to talk to me. Now too he forgave me when he caught sight of me, and he had tears in his eyes. He was rich, extremely rich. He had two houses in Prague and a magnificent villa in Beroun, what was the villa called? . . . Anyway . . . he forgave me and said that, if we would only live to see it, it would be a drugstore such as the Republic had never yet seen. And he would let me manage it, or he would let me lease it. That's how it was. After the war was over, in April, pharmacists were needed for the frontier regions, and I made myself available. At the time I was his manager. They offered me a number of drugstores. But my wife and daughter didn't want to leave Prague and he kept saying, 'Don't go, I'll lease you the store!' He liked me, had complete confidence in me, and could count on me. I knew all the suppliers' representatives, was friendly with the physicians, and was able to procure things. We had all the doctors in our pocket, and the hospitals gave us their business. So I stayed in Prague. Then quite unexpectedly, at two in the morning, they announced on the radio that the pharmacist in Jinonice had died and they needed a replacement for him at once. I went right away to the People's Committee, at two in the morning. I had outstanding recommendations. They let me have the job. They say he was angry at me, that I hadn't taken the time to talk it over with him in person. But, of course, I did write him a letter. He didn't reply at the time, but just now I've been to see him: he put his arms around me, he wept, said everything was fine, that the Republic had never yet seen such a drugstore as the one he would have set me up in."

Sitting, he spoke with bowed head, his eyes behind their round spectacles only rarely darting upwards. He wiped his forehead with his hand.

"I couldn't sleep at night: I sleep badly. I thought
of you—that you're in the film business. I know
people from there. One is pale, tall, with a moustache under his nose—what's his name?—he's a director. Vavra? Yes, that's probably it—Vavra. Is he a
director? Doesn't he come from that miller's family?
There in Čerčany, right by the station near the
bridge, there's a big mill—the name Vavra has always been on it. I come from a miller's family too,
from Southern Moravia. I'd like to live in the open
air—it would remind me too much of my illness if I
were to go back to a drugstore, the way they run
them nowadays—I couldn't stand to watch it. I
thought you might be able to give me some advice.
My friend Ulrych—he was at school with me—has a
drugstore in Ústí and sings there in the opera as
well—your wife might possibly know him. He's a
bass. The theater people respect him. I thought I
might try something like that—probably not going
on the stage, though, at least not right away. The fact
that he's in the theater and is a pharmacist gave me
the idea. I do have a great deal of specialized knowledge, and I could be of use. I could make myself
useful in that sort of film-making. While recuperat-
ing, I happened to visit my home town. I did some
work there, loosened the soil around young trees,
and even went out into the fields. We all liked it

there and I'd sing to myself. You know how it is. I would need to be in the open air some of the time. Maybe they could make a film like that. Maybe you're familiar with those humorous stories by Tůma, the ones about life on the road—what do they call them?—the people go from mill to mill and everywhere they go people are full of good spirits. If they ever made a film like that, I could work as a guide or a consultant, or I could simply show people through the places. The mill I come from is still standing, maybe we could even go and film it. It has eight waterwheels—it's a real giant. And the construction is ancient, it's of Turkish construction, all in a circle, with galleries. It's from the time when the Turks laid siege on Vienna. When it came into Christian hands, the new owner built an upper story with a cross on it, and that's still the way it is. I could show them that. But I know other things too, I have specialized kinds of knowledge. I could be of use, you know: I don't want to give in to it, I still want to live. The employment office of the Party called me about a month ago and asked me why I hadn't contacted them for a whole year. I told them I'd been sick, and that softened them up a bit. But I wouldn't like to go back to a drugstore, I'd like to be in the open air for a while. They want to put me on disability. Do you understand how that works? Can someone collect disability and a salary at once? I thought that's how a film could work. I could maybe be of use in the same way as Ulrych is a pharmacist and he's in the opera. Couldn't somebody film one of those Tůma stories? People would find it amusing. I could show people that mill—it's an interesting old building, unique in every respect. But please don't say anything to my daughter or my wife. If you should. . . . I've held you up, haven't I? It came to me when I couldn't get to sleep, the idea of working in films."

He got up slowly. I had hung his coat up on a hanger in the hallway, but he still had his hat. He took his coat and held it, but he was still gazing at the floor: he wouldn't leave.

"At the swimming pool in summer, on vacation, they asked me to perform and they were really amazed. They called it 'figure swimming.' We haven't got a sport like that. We could use something of that sort."

He put down his coat and placed both his hands flat on his right cheek.

"I can sleep, so to speak, this way on the water. I can hold myself for a long time or do all kinds of circles and other such things. Maybe I could be a trainer, if they needed something like that. Or, I thought that maybe you'd make a film of *Rusalka*, and I could be the watergoblin. It always made an impression on them when I would do that in the pool on vacation. That sort of thing ought to be called 'figure swimming.' But please, don't say anything to my wife or my daughter. And would you let me call you some time? Will you make inquiries? I thought of you when I couldn't sleep at night, and that's why I took the liberty of coming to see you. I don't want to let go so fast; I need to spend some time yet in the open air; I don't want to have to watch how they get rid of people these days."

I handed him his cane, which he had forgotten, hung up on the handle of the window, and we took leave of one another.

The Vedantist

"Here, I've brought it back. I kept it too long, and I'm ashamed."

He placed a small book from his briefcase onto the corner of the desk. It was bound in canvas and the pages were typed on a typewriter.

"I wanted to ask your permission to let me continue to translate it."

He hadn't sat down yet, but was leafing through the book. To do this he bent far over the desk. He was wearing strong prescription glasses, and had thick, wavy, slightly gray hair, rather long in back. His narrow shoulders, encompassed by an antique coat, were raised stifly aloft. He was leafing through, alternately raising the pages to his eyes and putting them down.

"Tell me, please. This passage isn't clear. There seems to be an error in the original. It should read 'small-lettered,' when it actually says 'large-lettered.' Huxley says here: 'look alternately at the name of the month in your pocket calendar, printed in large letters'—but correctly that would read 'small letters'—

and then, 'look at the name of the month on the wall calendar.' It isn't a perfect translation, obviously. So, shouldn't I have come to you for help? I want to test it according to his method."

He sat down on the edge of the chair, supporting himself on one elbow, with his fingers clasped. His body was bent forward, and he was compelled to keep his chin a bit higher in the air than was natural to him, for he had attached a semi-stiff white collar to his pink-and-white striped shirt. His wide-striped tie had not been pulled tight, but only closed at roughly the middle of the opening between its two sharply pointed ends.

"My translation is obviously incomplete. I have time to work on it only on Sundays. I was able to finish just this one chapter—the most important one. You don't happen to have a photo of Huxley, do you? Last time you told me he lives in California and that he also owns a villa in Aix-en-Province, that he has enough money, and a wife who's Belgian. And now, maybe, he's no longer wearing glasses? I'd like to put his method to a test. But how could you do it working in an office? You forget. You forget the most important things, even. At eight you're at your desk and at five you leave. They won't let you have visitors any more—only people from outside Prague. We have two supervisors there, one of them is quite decent, I know, he calls me whenever someone comes in, and even if we talk a whole quarter hour, he puts it down as just five minutes: They have to write down how long every visit lasts. But the other one doesn't even mention it to me. I work in the Discount Bank—it used to be the Land Bank. I've gotten away from interfering with work that way, but even so, it's a strange life. You forget about things, even important things. It often happens that I get home and only then remember that I was supposed to stop by somewhere, or take care of something. So what can I do about spiritual things? That's the way life is now. In place of the workers they sent off to the factories, they gave us girls to be trained. It's one long question after another. All day long I spend all my time answering their questions. In clearinghouse transfers there are all sorts of complicated things. And those girls aren't ready for them. Their heads are someplace else; they'd rather be outside somewhere. Those questions of theirs, they create more work. But perhaps it's what the regime wants, that we have no time left for spiritual things. The material structures, the dams, the factories in which they see the realization of their plans—this is what they present to us. But that isn't the real goal of life. I often wonder how ready people are to submit. Every so often some statement comes out for us to sign. Recently, for instance: It was established according to our norms that our division had to exceed our quotas by a hundred and fifty percent. They claimed it wouldn't mean any more work for us because we're already fulfilling by a hundred and fifty percent. Everybody signed it—only I didn't.

"I'm amazed at how easily our people give in. Churchill was right when he said that five percent of Czechs are scoundrels and ninety-five percent cowards. But maybe it's all planned that way. Everything that surrounds us: where we live, people, including the people among whom we live—all that is our karma. Our destiny, you understand, according to Hindu philosophy. The total repayment for all the acts we've committed in our past lives. And for as long as we go on being born into the world, so long will our life repeat itself until we achieve that fulfillment, that merging with the universe. But where can you find time for such things today? It often happens with me that in those long hours I forget what it was I wanted to do. It's those questions, always the girls' questions. And that laughter of theirs. They'd rather be someplace else. Like the other day. I simply couldn't put up with it, I begged her, I reprimanded her. I was forced to complain about her. Besides my work I have to answer their questions, all the time. I lose track of things during the longish hours. I forget to take care of myself, to think about spiritual matters, I have only Sundays left for that. And then not every week. Something comes up: I have an old mother who often gets sick, and I have to take care of this or that. It all may well be a plan to distract us from spiritual things. They build nothing now but material buildings; that's the goal according to them. And people submit to it. We really are a strange people, maybe. It's all a component of our karma.

Some people, most people who are part of our world are still not awakened, and some are awakened only a little, say half. They don't know, they don't suspect, they fumble in the dark. Churchill may well be right. And it is convenient for those who rule us that people are not awakened from that sleep, that *maya* that envelops us. Recently I've been reading—only on Sunday, otherwise I can't even think of reading, sometimes I get home and fall asleep at the table before Mother even has time to get supper ready—I've been reading a book, one translated by a Mr. Šimák, who lived for a long time in America. It's a report on a group of Vedantists in New York. It has excellent definitions as to what the true awakening is, the waking up, the final state of merging with the Universe. Mr. Šimák himself lent me the book; he's an extremely good-hearted person. Do you suppose then that there's an error in the original? Maybe there is. It could be because of the fact that, unlike the other writing on the wall calendar and in the pocket calendar, the letters of the month names are upper case. But the conditions are too unfavorable. It often happens with me that I go home and simply forget something. Those girls don't do much work anyway, their heads are elsewhere, they're simply passing the time. I even had to make a complaint about one of them. They transferred her to production. It's all a part of our karma."

The Trainees

All week long they give lectures about building bridges, houses, roads. On Saturday there's a different course of lectures: on how to destroy it all. The dark floor, the dead air, the green, painted frames of the dirty windows, the chart with its worn away geometric designs—as if this weekend took place in the half-excavated ruins of a lost civilization. Soldiers do the lecturing and twenty-five or thirty men listen, sleep, or think their own thoughts.

The Pastor

He sits on the front bench by himself. His hands are clasped underneath his chin and he looks out at the lecturer with slow, narrow eyes.

—The Scriptures say: you will have the patience of doves and the cunning of a serpent. In this world it's a relief to have such counsel at hand.

The Secret Agent

He's found a spot for himself by the wall. From dark, severe clothes a thin, haughty mouth looks out.

His eyes classify reality into the useful and the dispensable. Constant tension, held tightly in his fist.

—Go for whatever pays off.

The Grave-digger

All features point downward: the eyebrows, the mouth, the wrinkles along the nose. A pasted-on smile of aged reconciliation. It will never light up again, and never go out.

—One could hardly say what people go to such trouble for. And only a hole in the ground waits for them.

The Eternal Shop Assistant

Always willing to bow and mumble affably. The crumbs he lives on are in everyone's palms—but how to extract them?

—Come again. We'll have butter tomorrow at ten. I'll save some for you, of course.

The Son of the Genius

He is constantly reaching into his pockets, as if he had forgotten something. He left it at home, right in view, but he's forgotten to take it. A high skull with bright soft hair, gentle childish features. Someone who came before has lived for him, and his childhood has remained eternally in the shade.

—Look at the head I've got. Why? Who gave it to me?

The Unrecognized Napoleon

A protruding chin, carrying a face constantly on the lookout. He listens and assents with a nod of his head, dissents with a shake of the head from side to side. His reply is always ready on his lips. He cannot tolerate being left alone.

—Let me at it, whatever it is. Or it will be too late.

The Beast of Burden

He sleeps with bent back and face hanging down over his sunken arms, propped on the table. He wakes up with the ugly taste of a gray, long, dull weariness in his mouth.

—Forget, sleep.

A Playboy in Extremities

His curly hair has thinned. What used to entertain him no longer does. His carefree features are covered with a layer of fat. One gesture is left him: his hand straightens his necktie and his chin rises and moves from side to side.

—Heavens, it's still three. And then what?

King Lear

Everyone tells lies to him. He responds with tightly clasped mouth and closed eyes. He sees what is his. He does not look aside anywhere. Stiffened, he hangs on until the end: he waits haughtily until everyone has disappeared, and comes out alone, the last, but secure.

—They all lie and try to trip you up.

The Puppet

He had his hair cut short, and his ears are like wings. He blinks, raises his eyebrows, lifts the corners of his mouth. The nerve wires jerk within him, and he twitches.

—Tralala, tralala, tralala.

The Born Warden

He sits with his whole body stretched out; he would rather have had a higher chair. His glasses are a telescope, his fingers keys to the cells, his nose a barrier. He is in a temper because a gang of prisoners pays him no attention.

—We need radar on our heads. We need to know when they are escaping. God is a poor director for a prison. Let people think freely, and look what happens!

The Passenger

He props his face on his palm and looks out the window. From time to time he lurches to one side, as if he were resting in the dining car after his lunch and the express train were passing over the switches in a country station. But the landscape does not let him in. In vain he tries to press forward the lie that he is riding. The motionless empty wall out-side the window reflects the tormenting emptiness within.

—I can't bear stops. And she won't understand why I refuse to go with her to see her mother. On that Sazava local!

The Official

The indispensable pullover, and on top of it a necktie, like an arc of spouting water. His time has passed and he won't be president now. So it is time to get fat and not take anything seriously. He sits with the base of his spine on the edge of the chair, with his hands in his pockets, spread way out in front of him.

—As if I didn't know this queerly ordered world: at each tiny step a person must pause and sit.

The Phenomenon

For hours at a time he feeds himself and pulls the sausage casings out of his mouth. Victoriously he looks about like an idiotic lion that has easily crushed an inconsequential baby fawn. A man in his own territory anywhere. He always knows he is worth more than the others: It makes him feel good to be among them as a confirmation of this fact.

—I don't understand why he's so puffed up, that lecturer, as if he thinks he is better educated than me. I know everything he knows.

Don Juan in Retirement

He's hidden in back by the wall, the crown of his head inclined backward; his roaming eyes gaze at the ceiling. The grayish black stubble on his face will soon have to be shaved. His bare head shines dully. His forehead is lightly wrinkled with a grief no longer contemplative. The world on the whole has given

him a pleasant weariness. Now it is enough to lapse
into foggy dreams.

—For supper I'll go to the Golden Chapel. The
waiter is holding my place. "How many of you will
there be?" he asked. How many! A corner for one
with a view of the faded walls will do. My flower
bed is opposite, in full bloom. Each flower is in her
prime. I remember her and she exists. Or is it rather
that I have nowhere to go, so that no new one may
emerge? That's funny, I know the horrors too well.

The Child of Fortune

He smiles with thick lips. With a pencil in his
fingers he knocks slowly, softly, and regularly on the
table. He does not fear marking time, and time flows
along pleasurably. He has thrown one leg over the
other and goes on listening, as if what he listens to
were a sweet, tranquil, gently stirring passage from
Dickens.

—They always tested me at a blackboard like this
one, and it always came out well. Everything will always come out well up to the velvety closing of these
extremely tired eyes. Sister, thank you.

The Sod

He gnaws at himself. He starts with his nails. He
looks about crazily to see how much of him remains.
He leans so heavily that the table begins to slide. He
draws the table back to himself and with it lowers
himself from his chair. He gets up, laughs loudly,

and looks about for applause for his performance. Nothing. He gnaws on.

—Who managed to tempt me away from my home and my garden on General Street, when I've set dough to rise there for a tart with jam made from last year's currants? Why am I here? As always. Not only here. For the sake of a tiny square of land with currants and carrots? For the sake of Stázka, who doesn't cook, let alone bake? Just so she doesn't die? And on top of it all . . . I don't know why . . . I've got to shoot at someone, or whatever it is that fellow up at the lectern is saying, because he himself doesn't have any idea, evidently, why he's here. Not just here: in general. That's the worst of it. And he's not supposed to discuss it. He pretended he didn't notice the way I fell out of my chair. A sick head— sicker than mine. My neighbor on General Street told me, "Josef, you're a sod, but one can get along with you and count on you." Maybe one can, how would I know? Only those on the street know: my wife Stázka, our neighbor, a few persons here and there. But not the one behind the lectern. What could he know, the one who let himself be hired to kill people?

☆ The Face
Of Civilization
☆

Military training again. This time at the law
school. As soon as we had signed up we were sent
out, into the cold beneath the cadaverous statue
above the Czech Bridge and from there on still farther. I held out for a whole hour.

Most went on sitting. But not all. Out of a thousand, five or six of us went away. Why didn't more
leave? The doors were open, the heads above their
uniform collars blunt, the hours endless. Still they
didn't leave. They crouched and cursed, wearing
empty, bored, sleepy faces; but they stayed. The picture of a civilization which ended where it should
have begun: yellowed, wrinkled gray heads protruding above school benches, faces all turned in the
same direction. It might have helped them to turn
their backs to the achievements of modern military
technology in an unbound edition of just five or six
copies.

*　　　*　　　*　　　*

News came today concerning the one who went off in 1938 and lived through civilization and technology in its true aerodynamic, concrete, and death-dealing version as a navigator. His wife wrote: He is making trips to Milan, Rome, Paris. He purchases patterns from designers for fabrics in the employ of the firm of Ascher in London (up to 1938 it was located in Prague). Perhaps civilization begins to enter life at the point where the eyes have something to take pleasure in.

The Man on the Ground Floor

He has a round head with protruding ears, his eyes revealing greed long since sated. In the evening he sits at the window of a ground-level apartment; behind him one sees a curtain above a sofa. It bears a shabby sphinx and pyramid on the background of a pale red sky. He is just coming home, from the tailor's workshop. The needle and a long thread are his daily prayer of reconciliation. It always works. In the evening he sits and waits until night comes. When he goes to bed, he gazes at the light of a small electric bulb that, ever changing, penetrates the water in an aquarium. Both he and the fish would forget to live without that light. On the walls of the room, over the face of the sphinx, over his face, the illuminated water tank casts lightly undulating reflections. The whole room turns into a tank in which dumb bodies drift here and there, gaze with eyes long sated, sink into sleep.

The Chairman

What has happened? Didn't you listen to the radio yesterday? What did the news say—how is it going with him? Better, you say? Thank God. Imagine what a catastrophe it would be. It's all ready; just get the proceedings started. Our large-flowered begonia is there at the head, just opposite the Footpath of Peace. I had a large plaque made for it with the name Emily. You've got something to be proud of, now that they've named it for you. Everyone says so. Only Jeřábek with his old-fashioned roses is sulking. He claims I'm pushing forward too hard. It was Trubec who told me, the one who grows scarlet runners. He's making a nuisance of himself. So I put those azaleas of his right off by the entrance. He had himself photographed there with them. We must do that too, Emily. With our begonia. But right there Kubec was lurking with his stunted lindens. We mustn't photograph that. Don't worry, I myself will tell the photographer to watch out. He left the meeting offended, and called me a dictator. I, who have been so careful not to let things get out of hand in the top echelon. Emily, you hear what I'm saying? I who have been so careful. But I will go forward only if nothing happens to him. What do you think it was? A heart attack? That's bad, that really could turn out badly. So much work and bickering and then everything comes to naught. Again we'd be in mourning and everything would be lost. And we can't wait, it will all wither. I may give up the job. Do they really say that would be an improvement? You're sure you didn't misunderstand? Just think, thirteen foreigners are to come; we've planned a formal dinner for them; we'll serve duck. You know, I was only thinking of you. And now things may all go down the drain. You think that would be better, don't you?

The Topic

It may be that he's a man of the times. Everyone wants to cast a shadow behind him, especially if it's made of bronze. Long ago he would dream of how he could make his village famous. He was on good terms with the priest, but the priest was shiftless and only took care of a red, green, and yellow beehive behind the parsonage. "You should go to the higher authorities; I'm only a humble servant," he'd reply. And the dream of a place of pilgrimage would slowly be eclipsed by the idea of boy-scout jamborees in a nearby valley. But the leaders in Prague had their own minds, and so there was nothing left but to turn to the older idea of a parade using marching bands. Each year. Or perhaps rallies of country cavalry, a festival of magicians, motorcycle races, floral competitions, a conference of Esperantists, a get-together of birdkeepers or a tournament of deaf and dumb sportsmen? The war brought a decision. Two wretched survivors, from a crushed force of partisans, took refuge in the town. Those who were hiding them took fright. The man with the dream was among them. They took counsel and came to a decision. They would not allow their town to be burned down, as Lidice had been. They resolved to kill the men they had hidden and throw them into the river, in that very valley where such a lovely jamboree might have been held each year. They carried out their plan, but one of the wretches, half-stunned, managed to get away. He was caught, and before he died, he revealed a great deal. A few men of the town were executed. The man with the dream cleverly survived. And when, after the war, there were celebrations, he came back to life again. He gained many followers and allies, when he proposed that the memory of the two partisans and their heroic supporters be preserved through an annual memorial service and a monument. The leaders of the parties argued over who should unveil the monument, on which a heroic citizen with a badly sprained right arm would hold up a poor fellow with a gigantic head. In the haste of the final preparations someone had left an axe lying in the poor fellow's lap. It might even have been a joke in memory of those who had helped the murdered partisan to his end. But it all turned out well and participation on the part of the public was enormous. When in the evening the minister from the capital was leaving, he said, through the window of his official car, "I haven't had such pastry in a long time. You say your wife baked it? Give her my warmest regards."

The Brothers Korec

I couldn't walk past them and not speak. Two of the three were sitting on the edge of a raised slag walkway along the dusty broken highway. Near them stood two young women who were pushing their baby carriages back and forth. One carriage was white, the other blue. I walked along the walkway. One of the men glanced at me. He was tanned, with a firm, large hand. I felt it in my own hand. We exchanged greetings.

"This is Jarka," said the one with the tan.

And I offered my hand to Jarka. Fifteen or twenty years ago, we had run barefoot in the warm dust of this very road. In the yards we had worked at threshing. We had climbed through the barns.

"And this is Bohouš," the tanned man, whose name I couldn't recall, said. Awkwardly, I turned to the third man. He was sitting in a wheelchair. He had been famous. I recalled the hot summer noons, a green military plane circling over the village. On its wings were circles formed from red, white, and blue wedges. It had come down low. Its wings had shook.

Around Milovice, twenty kilometers away, there had been large-scale training maneuvers then. You could hear the firing from this very place where we were standing, on the edge of the raised walkway along the dusty road. The slag had pricked our bare feet.

"That's Bohouš!" someone cried. "Look, that's Bohouš Korec!"

I looked at the man in the wheelchair. Under his gray jacket he was wearing a handsome French white-and-blue striped polo shirt. Under it he had on a shirt and tie. His left hand, resting helplessly on the edge of his seat, ended at the wrist. He looked almost nothing like his brothers. He was much fatter than they were. His mouth was sunken in like an old man's, as he chewed on something. The scars on his face remained strangely motionless.

"Don't you recognize him?" the tanned man asked.

"How could he recognize me?" Bohouš said slowly. His forehead had many wrinkles and his eyes were peaceful. "Of them all I had the least idea why I should rush into it. And now I've got it. Fished out of the English Channel." The corners of his mouth were raised ever so slightly. "But things happened." With an effort he pointed with his stump past the white and the blue baby carriages to the far-off, low beginning of the sky.

The Night Before
Sunday School

—I squint a little; I've got pimples on my face; not just like other people, I've got them all the time—when some dry up, others come out ... My friends, everybody I know, is more important than I am, no one less ... Eda Polcar is district controller in the labor office ... Venda Šimán got a job on the newspaper *Pramen*, he's the top man at the big building on the main square, the one the Nováks occupied ... Střípek, ever since the time he was in a train crash as an engineer, has had trouble with his leg, it healed badly; he gets a pension and in the bargain earns extra money for working in garages; he fixes cars and they pay him because Střípek knows how to do it and everywhere else they charge more ... Everybody has it better than I do ... Lord, why shouldn't I accept my due when it comes to me, What's the harm in it, maybe it's the way they laugh, but I must study, I must read ... *And on the morrow, when they were come from Bethany, he was hungry: And seeing a fig tree afar*

*off having leaves, he came, if haply he might find any-
thing thereon: and when he came to it, he found nothing
but leaves, for the time of figs was not yet* . . . I must pay
attention in case somebody tries to snatch it up, but
Pastor Podhajský definitely said he would see to it,
he'd clamp down . . . from our district for twenty
years now nobody has studied to become a pastor
and our congregation is a big one, our church is the
most beautiful in Bohemia . . . Few people have as
much respect for me as Pastor Podhajský does . . .
Why is it, I wonder . . . I lead the young people, that's
true; I go to the sacristy every Sunday afternoon to
play ping-pong; I took him the food that Mama bare-
ly managed to scrape together—all true—he had eight
kids, she used the food up, but why he thinks so
much of me, for God's sake . . . I squint, I've got pimples . . . Perhaps it's because I praise his sermons, or
because Mama took care of him as long as she lived;
she did the cleaning for him, wheeled the kids around,
brought him eggs . . . but he can't want everything for
free, when he climbs those steps up to the pulpit I
always think, should he stumble, fall down, maybe
even break a leg, I'd run up at once, I'd be the first
he'd see in his pain, the pain that would be the end of
him . . . Now things aren't so certain. Will they send
me there so I can wash it away, scour it away, cleanse
myself of that smell, mostly the barnyard, the stinking
barnyard with manure . . . Dad was a farmhand and
tended the oxen, he had always wanted to work with
horses, Lord, how he wanted the horses and not the

cattle shed, he never mentioned it but he did want it, not just the dungbarrow, the dung, the pump for the dungwater, the treacle cauldron, the straw, the fermenting silage under the eaves, he wanted horses with leather reins, not just a couple of cows with a rope and wooden collars . . . But the grooms were young, none died, none went away, Dad was small, bowlegged, he squinted like me . . . and the window looked out on the barnyard, the only window, whereas outside, on the street, as it was called in the village, where there was a row of cottages with green gutters, with a slag walkway and with muddy ruts in the middle, an empty and deserted street, that way only a narrow, mud-streaked tiny window looked out and right by it hung a color print, Christ with the red heart on his breast, a Catholic color print . . . When was it that Mama took it into her head to convert to the Czechoslovak Church? Oh yes, I must have been around twelve, she was going to town to work as a maid, to the Podhajský's, that was the beginning. I must do something so that it will be clear, only why didn't Mama live to see it, she could have found out more, if Podhajský really wanted me to go there, to study theology, me, good Lord, after whom they always shouted, Karel's on his way to Hell, the Devil's chasing him with his shitty stick, Mama should have been here to ask him: God, when will morning come . . . *And Jesus answered and said unto it, No man eat fruit of thee hereafter for ever* . . . I have to comment on such a harsh sentiment, everybody thinks that

Christ is love, just as we have it written right over the door to the church, but I'll find out all about that . . . Good God, the emptiness around here since Hanka's gone, how could I have realized what she wanted, to be married to a bank official, honest, dutiful, hard-working, I'm like that too, why did she go away then, tomorrow I'll be at Pastor Podhajský's again, sitting, bent over my desk, Miss Kubištová will come, throw her tithing book on the desk, she'll jabber about Hanka and what she's up to, "I haven't seen her here for a while;" and "Karel, admit that she's in a family way," she cackles with laughter, bangs shut the glass door, she's a real witch, just as if she didn't know about it . . . Everybody knows I've been alone now for three weeks, with the stag on the green mat on the wall, with the bedding and one blanket; Hanka locked the next room and said she'd send for the things. What should I do? First I've got to know how it will all turn out, but she'll certainly come back when she finds out I've got a paid scholarship to study in Prague . . . Not everybody can boast of that, but Lord, I don't understand how they can give me one, I've only got elementary school and two-years of commercial school, Pavel Srb's finished regular high school, and he says to me, "Karel, don't be silly, you've got nothing waiting for you there, so why do you go to Pastor Podhajský's and to church"; I reply, I go because of my old woman, you know, she thinks she can't make do without it and dinner is always at two o'clock on Sunday, so I can hardly make the soccer game". . .

That's Pavel, at times I meet him by the church, this is
how he talks; he worked his way up to caretaker of the
storeroom at the railway station, while nobody will
ever promote me, I didn't join the Party . . . I squint a
little, I've got pimples, and I wonder at Podhajský, I'd
bawl, but no, tomorrow, tomorrow it'll probably
come, I'll get the scholarship, I've got as far as Mark, I
must read . . . *and when evening was come, he went out
of the city* . . . Good Lord, to get away from here,
Kubištová'll be by again, just as if she didn't
know . . . I'll lower my eyes, creep along by the wall,
escape here, or on Tuesday, Wednesday, Thursday,
and Saturday evenings to Pastor Podhajský's, to enter
the accounts for the tithes and collections, write letters, wait and wait until he finally says, "It's come";
but all that comes is his wife, fat, bedraggled, in a dirty
apron, she's brought cold rolls, she's wearing a smile
as big as if she were serving a goose, and she says,
"Eat well, Mr. Korec, my husband will be home late
today, he went to see Pastor Jiřičný at Loučen"; I'll be
left alone again, under the yellow electric bulb, it's
probably a ten watter, the kind they use in the
john . . . The pastor doesn't come, Hanka won't be
home again today, whatever did she think I could
make of myself when she married me, and Dad didn't
even come to the wedding, Mama didn't like to let
him go to town ever since the time long ago when he
went to the movies: when they were chasing the thief
of Baghdad over the roofs, he got up quite beside
himself and shouted, "Round the corner, catch him!"

and later Mama gave it to him at home, he could only gape, and he had to sleep in the storeroom . . . It's been a year now since the wedding and Hanka's left, by herself, without taking anything, she wasn't involved with anybody; a Podebrady waiter who worked at the Grand did lure Franta Kincl's old woman away, but mine, she ran away on her own, went back to Mama, who else would . . . *And in the morning, as they passed by, they saw the fig tree dried up from the roots* . . . Can anybody respect me the way Pastor Podhajský pretends to, how can I ever believe him after it all . . . Dad rose higher than the oxen, everyone I know is doing better, and morning is so far off yet . . . maybe Hanka escaped because of the stench that comes up from the water here at the farm when it's been dry for a while and the water stops running . . . Good Lord, morning, let morning come, I'll drop by at Pastor Podhajský's and ask if it didn't come yet; but no, that's silly, the mail doesn't come till ten and then I'll be sitting there, Kubištová, the old witch, will stop in and ask how Hanka's doing, as if everybody didn't know she had left home by herself . . . Yes, yes, yes, I'll study, Pastor, please tell me the truth, do you just need someone to watch the children Sunday afternoons when they play ping-pong, or do you think I could be a minister, me whom they call Karel on his way to Hell; read, I must read, maybe it's true after all . . . *And Jesus answering saith unto them, Have faith in God* . . . Franta Kincl's old lady was taken off, after all, by that waiter from the Grand, my old man got up and shouted . . . Mama always kept saying respect the good parson but if only she were here to tell me whether I should believe him too, that he doesn't just need somebody to write his letters for him, keep his accounts for baptisms, funerals, weddings, so he can go where he likes and have a good time; he's certainly laughing at me on the sly, Good Lord, and Hanka might come then and say she would do a better job there then that frowzy parson's wife, that she wouldn't let herself have eight children in ten years the way the other one did, that it would be better off for her with me, an educated theologian, than at home with her Mama . . . *For verily I say unto you, That whosoever shall say unto this mountain, Be thou removed, and be thou cast into the sea; and shall not doubt in his heart* . . . Pavel Srb says there's nothing promising in it, and that I'm old enough by now to have sense, but just let him sit down here by the mat with the stag, by the wobbly table, or just let Kubištová come and have a laugh at him, let him think who his old man was . . . and that view out of the narrow window, always muddy, onto the street with the slag and the green gutters, with the gate that creaks when no man but only the dog, the St. Bernard, has gone out, and on the door you see the fingerprints of those who use it, and beside the window a color print; it was there since before Mama joined the Czechoslovak Church: Christ with the red heart on his breast and a small flame above, a small yellow flame . . . God, if only Mama were still alive, she'd go every day to the pastor's, she'd have known how to beg him . . . *and shall not doubt in his heart, but shall believe that those things which he saith shall come to pass* . . . if it were only morning, I'd stop in at Pastor Podhajský's; no, that's silly, the mail doesn't come till ten and he'd only say, "Hello, Karel, don't forget to take care of that poster for the ping-pong tournament, but make sure it doesn't cost much . . ."

For Dreams That Now Have Ceased

Thanks, Nurse, no it doesn't hurt any more, don't worry. If only she'd leave, and not look at the rotting: the cowardice of flesh unable to fight against anything. I'll croak here. You can see it in their eyes—all of them. The old medical professor and the assistants. The nurse most of all. She's an expert in future corpses; nothing can ruffle her. She was in a sentimental mood. That's just the point. Just so they'd keep their word about what I asked of them: That no one call Marta or Mother. I'd have to pound it all out on the typewriter myself. Only that they should make the gate narrower, to the point of suffocation. But it has to go fast, before Marta or Mother starts suspecting what's up. They'll take a train, look up and down, stand here, look at this dried-up face, at the bandages, at the scars, and a thousand suspicions will come to their minds. It's as if a piece of me had disappeared—it's worse, much worse than if I felt it again, than if I heard it again.

It's worse to disappear, to disappear from the legs up, but still to be. It will be a disgusting sight. Through that yellow, blue, chopped meat the bones will stick out, the rags of bandages will hang down. Let nobody come, let them have me cremated. *Nurse!* She's not here, I've gone crazy. After my injections everything falls silent within me, but then all of a sudden I speak up. It makes you laugh. My right arm—I've still got it—I can raise it, I can lift it. The left arm—not so hot. A log. An empty space in a plaster cast, a blunt hollow tunnel. The left leg, the right leg, nothing responds, from the belly down and farther up as far as the left shoulder it's all a desert, dried up, sown with chips of ice, rotting inside. A mouse is running around there, a small playful mouse, it doesn't bite anymore, it runs, it plays. They mustn't come in, they'll see it. Hold back . . . slow. My right arm is still moving; I can still go crazy or not go crazy. I still exist. You can still argue again, you dumbbells, whether you should say "To be or not to be," or "To live or not to live." Come on in and try it. It's all the same, you idiots, all the same. How would I act now? Quiet, quiet, for God's sake. I've still got one arm, at least. Tears, it all makes you laugh. But how would I act? *Director, you promised me, remember?*—that if for a year or two we went away and acted in a provincial theater, you'd take us back again. Remember, it was at the school graduation party. He was sitting there at the head of the table; swollen, he puffed at his pipe. It was at the

Modranská Winecellar with the damp walls and a
waiter who was a poet. That day the poet Toman
was on the schedule. But which of the two Tomans?
Anyway. "They tortured me with medicines and
diet, / Until I thought to send them off to Hell. /
But now I long for blossoms / Red like blood with
its spell." He sat there. We didn't much care for
him. He had two or three favorites—the others were
nothing. I thought I belonged to the latter. I took my
chair and forced my way in between him and Sláva
Kobliha. He was always playing up to him. And he
said it to me there. One or two years and then there
would be a new theater and he would take us. At
that time he was only a director of plays and he
taught at the drama school. Today he's the general
director and manager of the theater. It wasn't a year,
it wasn't two. It was seven years. In the letter I
wrote, I should have called him Comrade. He was as
cold as a fish. I shouldn't have come. I smelled it on
his breath, he came closer, clasped hands, he had
cold, clammy hands, fish's hands. No, don't let anyone come here, for God's sake. I'll leave, down that
corridor, thank you, no, I won't take any, I'm going,
I've got to go. *Let go! You've got no right, you police
pig, long live President Beneš, down with Hitler! Can
you be Czechs, you traitor pigs? Can you be Czechs?
They're burying the Czech students, and you! Ha, ha,
you're bawling, but you keep at it. It isn't possible. So
long? No, then, I'll have a suit of sables . . . due two
months ago, and not forgotten yet? As the hobby-horse,*

*whose epitaph is: For, O, for, O, the hobby-horse is
forgot. Let me go. For, O . . . Who else . . . What's
that? No, thank you, thank you, Nurse. Just bring me
a little water.* To sleep, to sleep this way, that would
be nice. He promised it to her too, to all five of us.
She has a birthmark on her hip, and always, when
we were together, she would stretch her shirt over
that raisin in the cake. Květa, my Ophelia. When she
didn't have a shirt, at least a blanket. It was so tiny
pressed against the palm of your hand. With large
crazy eyes. Maybe I was asking too much when I
wanted him to take all of us. Květa, Franta Bílek as
Horatio, Pepík Stein as Laertes. And Svatava would
make a wonderful Gertrude. That was when I wanted him to produce *Hamlet* for our sake. I should
have called him Comrade. Now he's general director.
And it could be that he didn't even read my letter.
What was that bum from Carlsbad doing asking fa-
vors? Let him stay there. He looked up at me from
his desk with his fish eyes when I came in.
How . . . are you . . . nowadays? We're rehearsing all
the time, Director. Franta Bílek reads Horatio, Svatava the Queen, she cuts a figure, did you see Olivier's
production? She looks just like Herley. And Květa is
better than Jean Simmons. She's going with Franta
now, it's true, I gave her the boot when I married
Marta. Actually no, it all came back, it was so tiny in
the palm of your hand. Marta held me back. She'd
say, "Don't be foolish, Vráťa, you don't understand
these things." She'd say it's nonsense. But he'd pro-

mised it to me and now he just was just dragging
his feet. "I've seen you," he said. "You did a good
job with that play by Gorky." I should have told him
then what I thought about him. But he left, speaking
in the doorway, just when he opened the door and
the light came in, and then he walked out first and
left me there inside. He said he had to go. I felt confused and awkward as never been before, in the
doorway in the sunlight stood the great Krejča, a fine
actor, yes, he proved that. I shouldn't have insisted
that all five of us come. But no, I had to, I'd
promised them. He left me standing there. Krejča
was there, he knows how to handle those things.
They closed the door and I was left standing there.
When they closed the door, there was only the gray
office, his ink well, leather chairs, and the desk with
its papers and its empty chair. I dreaded the trip
back. Back to Carlsbad, again there, again there. I
should have spoken more familiarly, and called him
Comrade. But Krejča *was* better, I've got to admit.
Marta said don't go, she was in her bathrobe, it was
early morning, but I went. Mama, no! *Nurse, take
her away. No, I'm only acting, Mama, don't get
angry at me, no, I won't do it anymore, really I won't,
go away, I beg you, I'll get up, Marta, give me my
shirt from the wardrobe, the light blue one, Mama gets
angry when I eat breakfast in bed, let me go, I'll get
up, I must leave . . .* Let's have a cigarette, come and
lie down a bit, Květa. Come close to me again, that's
it. *No, Doctor, nothing hurts, just as usual . . . If I*

could just have a cigarette. Thanks. They disappeared down the corridor. I walked down the stairs and past the porter. There stood Jaroslávka. She said, "Hi, Vráťa, what are you doing here?" With her special version of a long *ahh*. As petite, as petite as Květa, but not as pretty. Fidgety though, eager for parts, a better actress than Květa. We are weak. It's true—I know it. Why did I come here? Only for the dreams that are now vanished. I left, and then I went back. There was time to catch the train.

How little I remember Prague. I thought that there would still be a café called Electra near the Museum. I wanted to sit down a bit. Large windows, illuminated brass chandeliers—I recall. But now nothing, only yellow walls and whitewashed windows. It was called Electra; the entrance was on the corner. And now only a wall, nothing but a wall and windows painted over. But both Marta and Mama would see inside. Under it, they'd imagine more than is actually there. Neither can come in. For God's sake no, Franta, be nice to Květa. *Mama, no, Marta isn't to blame, she's just unhappy—I was a pig.* Květa, come back to me. God, why did I marry Marta? Only a yellow wall and I was staring at it, looking to see where the entrance had been. From the Museum, tram No. 11 was coming down the hill. I had lead in my feet, I felt stupid for coming here, the shame of closing the door and coming. But yes, it was all right. Krejča here, me in Carlsbad, I admit it. No. 11 stopped with a bumping noise somewhere under the

vehicle, and the conductor leaned on his elbow behind the glass and looked at me. I was walking just
outside his window. His cap was tilted back. Then I
heard it. It was a Tatra, with its foreshortened snout.
A diesel, a 10-tonner. Pachovský from the bus line
always raves about them. The motor's the same as
that of a tank. I wanted to go to the Electra, but
there were only whitewashed windows. *No, today I
don't have to get up, Marta, there's no rehearsal. If
you're going out buy me a pack of Duklas, please open
my window. Yes, it's Carlsbad, it's you, Mama, please
connect us. Miss, yes, I'm calling Pilsen. Your ticket's
at the cashier's. Your train leaves at 14:30; you'll
make it. Franta, for God's sake, such a long corridor.
Walls, walls, walls.* When will we come to the door?
It used to be here at the corner. Nothing but glass
and wall and noise. He opened the door and the
light came in. And I knew they walled it up long
ago. For me, for all five of us. Only a wall and whitewashed windows.

The Music Theater

They are playing Honegger's Joan of Arc at the Stake. *There are one hundred members of the audience, each seeking to escape from his small material presence towards legendary self-enlargement, each with his own cares.*

After Dinner

People should have digestion take place outside of themselves. Like a motor. It would consist of a gear box, a brake, a tachometer. I must buy that model Spartak—next year's model. I'll talk her into it; we'll sell the lot and we'll always park it in front of the house. They'll be staring at us, the Škrdlants, the Pešeks, the Werners. It must succeed somehow. They're coming up with so many new things, but this they won't invent. The abomination of digestion should be located somewhere outside of us. She's always giving me something made with onions, and that's how it starts. Those who know medicine—they'd take notice. Dr. Žáček's artificial stomach.

Start it going at a suitable time so that the body receives nothing but pure, nutritious substances. That's how digestion has power over us, instead of the other way around. Life is unworthy when the stomach can torment us this way. It could be hauled through the side streets, but never to hear music. Everywhere there would be advertisements: Sleep in dignity with Dr. Žáček's stomach. And Pešek would sizzle with envy. What could he ever accomplish—a professor of history? He won't know how to classify it. He'll have to invent a term for the new era. And that old Catholic Werner will be saying: You're defiling the image of God. If only he'd leave me alone with that God of his. God knows why He gave us imperfect stomachs. For us to be aware of His presence. He's an old bureaucrat, He clings to His importance. Škrdlant would make a good partner— he knows his engines. He says the Spartak is just a tin can. But just wait and see how much we'll go up in price. We'll team up with a doctor who'll explain the digestion to us. It's revolting the way poor diges- tion gives a person bad breath. Where is one's digni- ty, where is art? I've got to run now and leave all the music to continue without me. Will it really happen? Please excuse me, I've got to go, excuse me. But no, I can hold out a while yet. From today on the artificial stomach will be my concern. It will be a struggle with nature and against the reactionaries. They'll drag me through the courts and call me a charlatan. But I'll give them nobility; I'll save them from their stomach torments. I'll defy their onion sauce once and for all. And she's got to let the lot go. Without a Spartak it won't work, they look on us as if I can't earn a living. Even if it costs me all my peace, I intend to go after it. It's so relaxing to think of important things. My indigestion is already getting better. Motostomachs can wait. No one can expect me to take a vow of poverty or faith like she has. Nobility and heroism are only words. The main thing is to show others that you are greater than they are. Digestion straightens out by itself. A Spartak will make everybody admire Žáček.

The Philosopher

Hello, is Mr. Honegger there? Good evening. This is Prague, the Music Theater. Spare me just a moment. I'm listening to your *Joan of Arc* right now. They're about ready to take her to the stake. She has fought the good fight; now they're making her a saint. The legend's just starting. I'm very impressed. It's warm here, the seat's comfortable, and there's a rather pretty young lady with me. We got to know one another a week ago. I still don't know too much about her. She's a bit bored, I can see, but she'll put up with it. Joan is just saying: "*Il y a de joie qui est forte.*" It won't last much longer. And my girlfriend's also looking forward to what comes next. We'll see what kind of person she really is. But tell me, Mr. Honegger, why precisely do we esteem Joan so high-ly, when she had to go all the way to the stake for

her great joy, whereas in real life we choose girls who
are so much more modest? And we too are more
modest. Even men can be the kernel of legend.
We're all born with the same opportunity and with a
hidden desire to become great. And then we walk
the streets in colorless clothing; we avoid danger;
here and there we make a gesture by which some
woman we admire might remember us, or some
man who is more important than we are, and we
seek his intervention on our behalf. Slowly we all
grow gray, and from the trip to the stake, which
could have made a legend of us, there remains only
the trip to the office, to the movies, a rendezvous, to
the Music Theater. Hello, are you still there? I'm almost afraid to tell you, but why shouldn't you know?
Were there a real stake in front of us and Joan upon
it, the result would be different today. You would't
have the strength to make her say it. We all go away
indifferent. The girl who's with me turned her eyes
toward me just as Joan's voice was breaking. She's
not afraid anymore, she's already halfway to Heaven,
and *she* says: "Let's go, all right?" I clasp her hand,
I'm embarrassed, but I have to go. There's always a
terrible crush at the coatroom, she'll be out of sorts,
and tonight I don't want that to happen. With each
day we are farther from our stake. We skirt it, keeping as far away as possible. I must go, she's so impatient. Why didn't you make it more powerful, so
that she too would be moved by it, Mr. Honegger?
Even she might become a legend. But we can only

manage the things we know. Without duration, for seconds, without eternity. And tomorrow, dull clothes on a dull street, life worse than a dog's. So what's there to do, what's music for? Now on top of it I can't find the coatroom check. So long, Mr. Honegger. You've ruined my evening. She was bored.

Mr. Šumpetr

I

At the Music Theater we watched Gershwin's opera *Porgy and Bess*. Earlier, before I left home, Milan was broadcasting Hindemith's *Chamber Music for Viola d'Amore, Piccolo and Orchestra*. The music of an experienced and beaten man. A distillation of a man's excitement and of his feelings; images, dreams, and figures projected in the cold form of ornaments and playful reflections, the artificial composition of a still life. A Vivaldi influenced by our times. After the initial impact the music and the rests sank back into their original forms, but with more confusion, more groaning, more disquietude, more anxiety. Then came a feeling of unfulfillment, as if someone had been dealt a high card before the game was to start which then turned out to be useless. On the other hand, Gershwin was playing with all his strength, even if what was available to him was not exactly the very best. Because there was a full house, we sat on the staircase. We sat behind some drapes,

which were pulled slightly aside, with a view back-
stage of the closed door leading to the auditorium. A
couple of steps down from us sat a pair of lovers; on
the right sat a young man in a bluish checked jacket
with a yellow scarf around his neck. There are pho-
tos on the wall of our composers: Vítězslav Novák
listens, the corner of his mouth drooping in contempt. Even in Gershwin, Suk hears his own angels
of death. Janáček alone has sparks in his eyes and
says that only now would the world see what he
could have done with such material. In the story, the
African-Americans love, amuse, murder, grieve for
one another and dream nostalgically of the promised
land. There is a corresponding groaning, hiccuping,
moaning, cantilenas of love and hateful convulsions
in the music. The same sort of melodies and
rhythms might have been diluted and commercial-
ized later in the jazz industry. Here they were in a
more authentic state; it was as if the light of a hot
day had replaced the colored lights of a revue.

Beneath the low, white ceiling of the buffet the
listeners met one another. There nostalgia for a
promised land was transmuted into coiffures, necktie styles, into leg positions within narrow skirts. A
Prague "Little America."

While the buffet was cleared away, a man lingered
at a table near the counter, stooped over, with a dark
ribbon instead of a necktie beneath his dirty collar.

"What is it you're writing today, Mr. Šumpetr?"
asked the girl who was cleaning the mugs with the

brown dregs and the glasses with red rims from the ladies' lips.

"A treatise, my girl," the man put his pen down upon the sheet of paper on which he was writing.

"You'll go crazy if you continue to write every day they way you do."

"No one wants to talk to me, so I write."

"And what's it about?"

"You wouldn't understand, little girl. It's a treatise about a new recording system to enable everyone to record their part at home. It takes a great deal of effort to pull together: the streetcars can get overloaded, heels can be worn out, the tenor can get laryngitis. Just look at the mob that was here tonight. It struck me right off. No, my girl, according to my system everyone will stay at home and do their playing and singing there. Then the sounds will all be put together. Just think of the orchestra. The players will play in the comfort of their own homes, and the conductor can't get angry at them. He can synthesize it all in the comfort of his home."

"But why do you do your writing here, Mr. Šumpetr?"

"It's cold at home, my girl, and I'm all alone there."

"Goodnight, Mr. Šumpetr." And the young girl disappeared in the doorway behind the counter.

Again we sat on the stairs. Bess is dejected now that the strong man Crown has seduced her. Their affair is like an illness. The widow Serena tries to

cure her by casting a spell. The peddlers with their
crabs, vegetables, and fish begin to call out, selling
their wares. All the flowery phoniness of the usual
opera was absent. Perhaps this was because from
where we sat on the stairs we saw more than the
illusory scenery and makeup through the open
drapes. The girl in front of us lowered her head on
her friend's shoulder. Bess lets herself be tempted
by "happy dust" and leaves with a quite ordinary
scoundrel for New York. The black Eurydice disappears into the underworld. "Why cocaine?" the
head on her friend's shoulder asks. "But New York
would be all right—why not?" For some it is an underworld, for others it is a dream of excitement in
the earth's epicenter. Mr. Šumpetr entered into it
the moment he walked into the cold solitude of
home.

II

Yesterday I read in the paper that they are going
to record pieces of music with one instrument lack-
ing, so that each listener can play that part as the
soloist, a soloist who waits with ceremonial humility
until the conductor nods to him discreetly that he is
to play, just as if he were a member of the finest
string quartet, or as if he were Menuhin himself,
playing a violin concerto. I thought of Mr. Šumpetr.
He must have been the inventor. I had an idea, but I
didn't know how to get at it. Only he could advise

me. I guessed that at the Music Theater he would not feel sufficiently alone, since the noise of the intermission would be coming to an end, and so we decided to meet at the Savarin. In the entrance I saw that he was talking to a waiter. He was wearing the same ribbon instead of a tie and the same shirt he had worn a week before. It was just a trifle darker.

"There's no law about it, waiter, and you can't make me," he was telling the waiter.

"It's considered proper, sir, to order something when you go into a restaurant," the waiter said.

I stopped about three steps away from the table and waited for the outcome. A lady at the next table raised her bespectacled nose and looked intently from the waiter to Mr. Šumpetr and back again. Finally, after so many long days, she was being entertained. By the window with the yellow curtain, in back of which a streetcar was crawling toward the stop, a gentleman was snapping his fingers at the waiter in vain.

"I've written a treatise about it, I know what I'm talking about. Sit down and I'll explain it to you. But do sit down, it'll take a while. You see, that's another prejudice. Why shouldn't a waiter sit? All that's discussed in my treatise."

"But sir, either you order, or . . ."

"I won't. I'm no slave of habit. Where would I get with my invention, if I were to obey everything that's set forth? No, I won't do it. You don't know whom you're speaking with."

"Sir, I do know that, because I can see it. So order something."

"Illusion, waiter. What you see is an illusion. It's in my treatises, not in my look. You certainly haven't read my treatises on 'Chess for One Player,' or my 'O Lonely Man, Do Not Be Angry.' The possibility of arguments and quarrels is excluded, quiet is guaranteed, city nerves are treated without pills. Doesn't a person have two hands? All you need are two ribbons, say blue and red. You tie them on the wrists. Or maybe you'd be interested in something more intimate. 'Marriage for One' is my title and it has a supplement which I call 'A Honeymoon Without Baggage, or the Honeymoon at Half Rates.' I talk about husbands and wives, always in a special chapter. It's all from experience, none of it is made up. And before long you'll be hearing about my new way of playing music."

This I already knew about and, in any case, the waiter was losing his patience. I came up to the table.

"Waiter, two Turkish coffees."

"You're the man for me," said Mr. Šumpetr. "I'll do a treatise on you: 'How Not to Be Alone in a Café.' Two Turkish coffees and it's all set. Wonderful, sir, you're just the man for me."

"If you don't mind, one of the coffees is for you," I replied.

"You've disappointed me cruelly, sir. Just by the fact that you've joined me. I'd have been better off without you. I could have had a subject for a treatise: "A Meeting for One.' But what can I do? Sit down."

The lady nearby turned her head away and inclined it toward her magazine. The gentleman by the window waited until the waiter came. On the other side of the windows with the yellow curtains people flowed by, and in front of The House of the Child there was a long line.

"I was looking around there too," Mr. Šumpetr. "But that's done with. Long ago I wrote my treatise called 'Forming a line with One Person, or How to Get Crushed When You're by Yourself.' You've spoiled it now, but do tell me what this is all about, as long as you're here. I'm against all such customs as listening to anybody other than oneself conversing, but still, give it a try."

I explained to him why I had sought him out. He must come up with something. People are sometimes at home by themselves, but they feel like talking. Just like the records where one instrument is missing: The conversation plays and places are left open for the listener to supply his own answer. Without a word he picked up his briefcase, pulled out a sheet of densely written paper and rapped on it. It was entitled: "Four-Way Conversation for One, or Drink Up the Wine Yourself." He leaned over and began to read.

"Times are bad. There's no money. People are tired. They don't want to set out in the cold. They don't want to be tied down by responsibilities. If

they visit others, they must in turn invite those people to their own place. All that can be stopped. Let
the record companies consider. On average, four
people can easily drink two to four bottles of wine
in an evening. That comes to around seventy
crowns. If a recording of a conversation, one that
grows increasingly intoxicated, costs forty crowns,
and if the prospective host buys that record instead
of inviting his friends home, and along with the
record just enough wine for himself, in other words
a single bottle, he'd save something like twenty
crowns, and perhaps some of the wine as well. Success is guaranteed, especially when you take into
consideration what trouble guests give, that they
smoke the place up, and that you have to go down
many flights of stairs to open the front door to let
them in. The objection that a single record won't
last for more than one evening is without substance.
In our time conversations, especially conversations
that get increasingly more drunken, are all hopeless-
ly repetitive. And the host will have a better chance
to polish his remarks, for it's well known that very
often we only realize late the same night, the next
day, or even years later, what the clever response
was to something a friend said. Here is the only
possible way of to get to say the things one can't
think of right off the bat. A way that is guaranteed
never to disappear. I offer a selection of conversational topics from which the buyer can choose.
Humbly, Šumpetr."

So my idea was right there on paper. Before I took leave of Mr. Šumpetr, we agreed to work up conversational groups of three or four and then meet in exactly a week. But as for me, I was not to come, he added, that would spoil everything for him.

"You're actually the first person who has spoken with me," he said.

"But I didn't get a chance to say very much."

"But even so, believe me, I've never felt myself so much alone."

Three for Bartok

I

"Just try sending you to buy anything! I told you to look up Miss Řeháková at the Valdek ticket agency, so she could recommend something worthwhile, but you insist on doing it yourself. You've ruined my whole evening. Just tell me where you got the big idea. First thing, you couldn't hear anything; the phonies must have thought I'm here to strain my ears. And when I tried coughing twice, the lout in back of me grabbed me by the shoulder and told me to keep quiet. I paid good money, so I guess maybe I can do what I want! But it's all your fault, you didn't consult me and you bought tickets to hear some lousy Hungarians. I knew right off what was up. Forty crowns for the tickets and then somebody grabs me by the shoulder. I gave him a real hard look—he wasn't anxious for any more of that! You were there and you saw it. Nobody can take liberties like that with me! And after that he didn't dare! But next time it won't be you who goes to get the tickets.

When somebody takes it into his head to pound the tambourines, wail on some mysterious instrument, and pluck the strings on the violin instead of playing properly, then I'm not about to pay for it. We've got enough noise all day long on our own street. And if that's not enough noise for you, then go pay for the tickets yourself, but be sure you've earned the money to spend on them. You loll around all day long and then you bring me to this. And don't start bawling on me. You should have done your bawling before. There's the bell, let's go. Let's hope Beethoven won't be a stuffed shirt like this man, whatever his name is. Who's going to remember these Hungarians, anyway? Forty crowns, you could almost buy a pair of shoes for that. Let's go."

II

She leaned her bare elbow against the rose marble of the balustrade and lit a cigarette. The mirrors on the columns through which they pass to get to the coatroom multiply the figures. Some women obediently stop where the men stop. There are also women who proudly show off their hips and keep moving whenever they want to. The men with their hands in their pockets rock on their tiptoes. They amuse their wives or turn away from them to the side to look elsewhere. The mirrors multiply their gestures. There are an endless number of feet treading about on the carpet in the languid minute of emptiness. It strikes her that everyone is just waiting, like the crowded rows of coats in the coatroom, guarded by female Charons with gray hair and wrinkles in sunken cheeks, wrinkles from endless watching. They wait for their rebirth, for new blood, for fervent blood that will take them out from the embrace of long waiting to enter the excited paradise of awakened memories, or newly fresh feelings, of ecstatic moments experienced again. In each movement, each word they speak, each match they bring near the end of their cigarette, each look they cast on strange faces, and on the sickly flowers of the friezes and columns of that dead architecture, in each expiration and inhalation they anticipate that there will come a sudden warm cataract, a tense, blissful drama, a battle won in advance, life in the light and blue instead of life on Charon's shore. As she anticipates. Only now does it reach her. The music was the jolt that had pushed her here, to the brink of expectation. The introduction to a hundredfold experience. The system of mirrors, drawing the material of life in like a vortex and giving it out in a glowing, multiplied form that doggedly tempts, ruthlessly threatens, degrades, and invites, breaks into fragments and drives to seek a new shore. The bell rings, and clumps of people slowly start moving upstairs again along the two wings of the staircase. She stubs out her cigarette with the tip of her slipper and follows them. The aging Beethoven, which comes next, like Charon returns them to sleep without expectation.

III

"Look, Maruška, there are the Koulas. Good evening, how are you, Eminka? And Karel, what do you think? When are you coming to see us again, folks? Did you see the tennis match? How can you say that—it's not the same thing. When you think back to Jarda, you could just cry. Just imagine, I was supposed to go to advancement training today. I don't know, it'll end up some way. Listen, wouldn't you have a spot in your clinic there for a nurse? Do try, Karel. You know relatives. She's living in Hradec now and she's terribly lonely. What do you know, they're asking me to come back to the ministry as a cabinet member. I know what you think of that, but at least it won't go to somebody else. Anyway, I don't have a choice. You know, I don't practice anymore, I don't feel much like it any longer. Eminka, you look so pretty tonight. Why don't you ever come to see us? Are you mad at us? I was just telling Maruška how happy I'd be if you'd come. So you liked the Bartok? Come on! I expect the Fifth Symphony will take the bad taste out of my mouth. What shameless modernism! But I know you're pretending so you'll appear younger. Well, don't take it badly. How do you get away with that advancement training? I still think it can be useful. Oh no, nothing specialized. Come on, I'm fifty—what could they teach me. Political? So you don't go to that sort of thing? Well, I know you were always stubborn.

Eminka, tell him sometime that he also has a few friends, and come to see us. You're going to have a smoke, well all right. We'll say goodbye then. Did you see them, Maruška? He talks to us out of the side of his mouth. But I'll show *him*, a lab assistant in his fifties, if he ever tries to get anything out of me. Bartok, they like that. He'll pay for it, some day. I could have helped him out at the ministry now. That's his problem. Come, let's get back to our seats. I can't get that advancement training out of my mind."

Memoirs in a
Prague Gallery

☆
☆
☆
☆
☆
☆

Brueghel: *Haymaking*

He is standing with his arms crossed on his breast amid the walls of the old palace. He has wandered in on a run-of-the-mill afternoon. From the walls dozens of paintings stretch their colors and forms toward him. He has passed many of them by, unimpressed. Now he is standing here and it strikes him that it is all very much like an airplane taking off. The engines howl, the stick is almost on your chest, your stomach remains back on the ground—it resists. The airport is left behind while all around you is the undulation of ridges, woods, and settled areas. The earth is not yet flat and broad, but in a little while it will be. He would always wish to fly like this, less than three hundred feet up, to be over everything yet see everything, as if he were part of it. You could do that only during training, never with passengers. But for the past seven years: nothing. No light mist washing all the colors in the world with silver, flight neither low nor high, no stars or cities, no rivers or the snail-like vehicles on the highways, nothing. Vítovec, Petál, and Konvalinka go on flying: their reward for giving of themselves to the point of losing themselves. He could not do it. He should have flown away. But here he is, stuck to the ground, a casualty forever. Not death, but then not life either. With his pitiful pay as a night watchman in a cheap hotel and a long, empty yearning. Life would be just like in the picture, with the feeling of constant takeoff: he would go to his father's and work with him in the fields earthbound and rooted in the soil. But that isn't how it is: people no longer have the right colors or open faces full of expression, they no longer have the vigorous long stride of those three women with the rakes and the broad-brimmed hats, they don't rake hay while doing a sunny dance, they don't carry bushels of fruit on their erect heads. Only long, dull toil without white horses, without clouds changing as if in a dream into gigantic cliffs over the square. Father's hut stands up to its neck in mud. Father bears up very well; he breaks in, ferilizes, and rakes the fields himself. He could use his help. But isn't there a shining gray town in the distance over the river? The colored earth does not stretch toward the eyes as when you take off. There the world has become stunted into furrows and wrinkles, while elsewhere it has grown expansively. They sucked up the blood of the colors, the polyphony of the fields, perhaps even the light of the sun. There was left a hard journey from winter to winter. Only when you take off does the

countryside, even now, open its arms formed of light
and shadows: like a voice speaking during sleep it
partly unveils a mystery. Why do people remain
here? If only he could take off again; then, even for
him, the blood would come back to the colors of the
earth, as in this painting. He steps back a bit toward
the window, and behind him the stunted, thin vege-
tation outside is desolate, empty, motionless.

Rousseau: *Self-Portrait*
"Come here, Voldán. Do you see that thing there?
You have to look at it close up. A mug like that, and
the way they hang the painting—you can see it three
rooms away. Just forget the Sponge and let's get
going. Anyway he talks too much and they'll soon
put him in the cooler. Or at least he won't be allowed to try anything. Dad says he knows him from
the Počta Wine Tavern; they often sit together there.
Dad too trusts them the way a mouse trusts an owl.
How about yours? But don't go blabbing around
what I'm telling you here. They'll get square with
the Sponge real soon—count on it. Think about this,
for instance, he takes us to see the Frenchman, and
you remember how Rejtar told him then that his father, the writer and party member, was in Russia
several times and saw lots of wonderful pictures by
modern masters there. 'Buddy,' the Sponge answers
him, I wouldn't expect to hear that country called
Russia by you, in other words, something different
from what the place calls itself, an international
union of independent republics. And I've been to

that country and looked for masters there and discovered, unfortunately, that the galleries there have
pictures only from bygone times and other countries,
while artworks by their more recent masters have all
either been exported or never existed in the first
place. Any questions, anybody? Yes, of course, Tro-
jan. That's a good question. Evidently the painters
there didn't die out, they're just hiding out below
decks.' So Rejtar got his, but the Sponge likely did
too—another minus for Rejtar to enter in his black
book. I'll pinch it from him, and his little pencil, too,
I promise you. But on the other hand: poor Rejtar.
To have a party member for a dad would be too
much for anybody. With all that they managed to
destroy, both in people and otherwise, as Dad says.
One of Mama's brothers was in Germany during the
war with the delegation that took Goebbels that
painting of the Prague Castle in oils, and just for that
Dad slammed the door shut right in his face—he
wouldn't let him in the house. Anyway, that's how
he tells it to us at least twice a year. But he too must
like to show himself in a better light than he really is.
At least we can claim to the director that we didn't
hear anything when he starts interrogating us about
the Sponge. I like the Sponge, but to blab it all
around out loud doesn't make any sense. Remember, heavy sentences have been imposed, by the wisdom of our splendid masters, on those whoe merely
listen but don't then turn informer. Think about the
Soviet brat and stool pigeon Pavlík Morozov, for instance. Are you listening to me at all, Voldán? Look

at this painting. It actually resembles Sponge himself.
Not in the look, the getup he's wearing, or the soup
strainer. Just the way he stands: clumsy. Let's see
what his name is. Rousseau. But it isn't that Jean-
Jacques, Voldán. Just so on your account Grandaddy
Know-It-All doesn't double up with joy in history
class. But even so, it just could be Jean-Jacques.
Look at it. Another tenderfoot. Supposedly, everybody's good by nature. A *tabula rasa* or whatever
they call it, and human society inscribes its principles on it. And it's done a beautiful job. For instance, take that swine we all can recognize, Mr.
Petas from our building. Nobody knows what his
job is or where, but what he's paid for it is in his
eyes and his duds. Or take Pavlík Morozov, promot-
ed at the age of fifty-five, in the appropriate institu-
tion, like Dad says. But don't go blabbing that
around. Look here, that fellow couldn't have done
anything good. It wouldn't have occurred to him. He
wasn't smart enough. You know what I mean. Otherwise he wouldn't have gotten away with not knowing any perspective or being able to paint correctly
and yet he's hung up in a gallery with famous paintings all around. Or could Petas' would-be geniuses
get away with it too? They likely could. But to hell
with anybody who paints like that. Why bother to
think about him? That's too much for one poor
gallery and two high-school juniors. With this there's
more fun. Look how those puppet shoes are floating
over the sidewalk or whatever it is. He didn't forget

the ribbon on the sailor's cap, even if next to that
boat he does look like Gulliver among the Lilliputians. Did I say 'mug,' Voldán? Then the sailor from
that tollhouse has got to forgive me. You didn't hear
what the Sponge had to say about it. During the war
you couldn't bring anything into Prague, not to mention a live goose. If the goose in the suitcase hisses—
and when the train comes in, or on the road, the
customs officer won't take bribes—you could even
hang for it. *He* worked in the tollhouse outside Paris.
The world is a madhouse. Sometimes a customs
officer who takes bribes is a whole lot better than
one who doesn't. *He* very likely knew how to do
both, depending on the circumstances. At least judging by that mug, which isn't a mug, and judging by
the Sponge's speeches, obviously. What the hell,
Voldán, what is it I like so much in that painting?
Say something once in a while, too. You pop your
eyes like you were just born but it won't help you
say anything. Now I've got it: Just born, you take a
brush in hand and paint. That's it. With each stroke,
with each little flag on the boat, with each added
color from the palette on his thumb, he's newly
stunned that he's been born, that the world was born
for him, that here something is being born, something that had never yet been. Voldán, that must be
something, to take your brush, your paints, your
canvas and not be afraid whether people will praise
you or not. To let them all think what they want to.
I like that about Sponge. I'm sure he paints at home,

his stuff probably isn't worth anything, but he knows
you've got to get right down to business, and then let
everybody go after you the way owls do after mice—
they don't scare him. It's here and it's finished. Only
between knowing what needs to be done and actually
being able to do it there's a gaping hole. I won't let
any monkey business happen to the Sponge, ever—
I'll see to that. We're his last students. He's going to
retire after we finish school—that's why I don't want
him to remember us as packs of little idiots. I'll handle Rejtar in case he blabs anything to the director.
Hey, just look, Rousseau is another Sponge! Wooden,
naive, no perspective, but no one for centuries before
him could have invented what he did—or ever will
again. A new world. It came out this way, that's how
it came out, and look—think of something, or just
move away a bit. Rousseau himself, forever the only
one, even Rousseau as a piece of the Sponge or of
other honorable beings, unadorned, undeformed—
take me as you find me and that's it, I'm a new part
of the world and recognize me or don't recognize me,
it doesn't matter—I am. What society could spoil
him or improve on him? He's come into being and
knows what will be the consequence of that. Or real-
izes that he doesn't quite know that. No one quite
knows that. The cleverest people know it least of all.
But even if he doesn't know, he's got a brush, paints,
canvas; he poses himself along the embankment, next
to him the boat and little flags, he puts on a sailor's
uniform and it's all there. The new-born customs

officer. Colors, outlines, his own moustache and his eyes agape, the boat, the river, the bridge, the green slopes along the Seine outside Paris; awkwardly, from the first clear water. And even the powers that be, trained by those masters—those powers that do whatever they wish with us, they dare not take him down from the wall. Voldán, the Sponge is clumsy, and if he goes on thinking out loud in front of Rejtar and his kind, they'll kick him out before he retires, and he won't even be able to dig a decent grave with a shovel—it won't be us pushing him toward it then. Promise me, you mute mouth, that you'll help me if something unpleasant happens there. I'll take care of Rejtar Junior myself in case he'd like to blab something out. Look, they're already finishing up—let's go meet them and listen to what the Sponge is confessing now. Sometimes it's pretty awful, how he's asking for it, but don't make objections: for he's the one sailor in our staff of pedagogues. I'll let the director himself have it on the mug if he cans the Sponge even if they do kick me out of all the schools in this country. Anyway, Dad keeps saying: 'It's good like this, at least you'll get to know life.' No, he's not giving himself airs, he's almost completely straight. So, why shouldn't I have the luxury of liking one single educator from among the thousands of those from the East in all the high schools, universities, and one-room schoolhouses. Let's go and listen, Voldán, and if you blab, to me you'll be as bad as the director and both Rejtars combined."

A Father in 1947

No one questioned him; they all bowed their heads in the railway compartment, but he wouldn't stop and it was hard to put up with him. He sat on the edge of his seat, pulled the window up and down, went out into the corridor, and returned a minute later. He had three bottles of soda water over his head in the net, and when we came to the frontier at Cheb, he only stood at the open window with a bottle in each hand. We rode slowly over the highway crossing, between the barriers, and on the other side of them people stood and waited for the barriers to open. He threw one bottle at them and then a second one. They both fell into the dust of the road under the wire net of the barriers. We could see the Germans looking around curiously to see from which window the bottles had come. Then the German conductor arrived and the man with the bottles said to him, "Heil Hitler."

The conductor looked at the tickets and said nothing.

"I'm saying hello, can't you say hello too?" roared the man with the bottles.

"Sorry, I didn't understand you."

"Don't you even know who Hitler was? You should know who he was."

He pulled out his breast-pocket wallet and from it a photo of a young man in uniform.

"He killed him: my son."

"I was a Social Democrat," said the conductor.

"Sure, that's what all of you were."

"No, but I really was."

And the conductor pulled a photo out of his breast-pocket wallet.

"This is *my* family. There were five of us, and now there's only me."

"You people did it."

"No," the conductor said. I was a Social Democrat and a member of the Reformed Church."

I closed the door behind me. And the man with the bottles went on talking. Everyone in the compartment bent their heads.

"We've been in Chile and now I'm on my way back. I thought I would come back and kill him. But they wouldn't let me in the Castle. He knows how to protect himself. Guards and officials and arms. Do you think my son had all that? I hate him, and they all gaze at him and take off their hats. As if the president were another sort of being from me or my son. We were in Chile and they left us in peace. He was nineteen and he had to go. The English wanted the Czechs to go, and he was willing. I hate them all. I won't go back on an English ship—I'd set it on fire.

The Germans, the English, all of you. Where were you when they killed my son? All of you were Social Democrats, that's for sure. Members of the Reformed Church. All of you just think up excuses."

As the train passed by, he took the remaining bottle and flung it from the middle of the compartment at the flock of people by the ruins of the station. The bottle broke against the window frame. The shards of glass rained down on the bent heads in the compartment; some fell on the floor. He quickly snatched at the shards so that he could still hit those outside. He only hit wreckage extending and repeating itself along the track. The fragments cut his hand, so he sat down in his corner and sucked up the blood with his mouth, saying something incomprehensible through his fingers and palm.

"Tit for tat," someone uttered to the speeding rhythm of the wheels.

An eye for an eye, a tooth for a tooth, this is for that, and that for that previous instance whereby it came back, the original, the pre-original, the pre-pre-original business. In different ways that grinding on of the wheel of revenge points to guilt and innocence as more or less the same thing.

Operation Angel

It was three o'clock in the morning when they woke us up. Quietly, without a bugle, from tent to tent. The boys in the service whispered as if it were the real thing, and something of that indeed hung in the cool dim of morning, turned green, as the day started to rise from the tops of the pine trees. The frightened birds were the loudest, along with the metallic blows of the barrels on helmets and of cudgels on knees and elbows. Within ten minutes ranks were to be formed, and the officers adopted looks of determination, either to hide their lack of sleep, or from the impression that it was all for real and that in a little while we would all fall down whimpering, some of us with shrapnel in our bellies, after which we would burst out of our tanks to attack and the enemy would fire at us crazily lest they too should whimper. We had spent three weeks in the forest drilling and twice already we had seen real action, but that was in daytime, and we knew it was only a game to make something happen and to show that officers are really officers. This time it was night, close on to dawn, our dreams mixed into what was happening, and when we came out to the edge of the forest there were camouflaged tanks, brutes with foliage in place of hair. The foliage sparkled with dew, but their gun barrels stuck out and the grass around them was torn up. It all resembled a dream which all of a sudden acquires firm edges, the odor of damp clay, and above it a real sky.

The light of day slowly began to expose everything below, and that which was on the earth appeared defenseless and poor and blindly reconciled to all that was to come. To wear a helmet and carry weapons, to crawl up to the slippery metal of the tanks and hear the blows of rifle butts and barrels against tight armor plates and the whispered commands or curses when the officers were displeased at something, in all that there is always a piece of the grave and a piece of awareness that we are in an enormous trap and there is no way out. The tanks had started up and the racket performed wonders, we could talk inside the tanks and nobody would hear us and all the subtle smells vanished and there was no time to identify them in the wave of diesel fumes.

The day was beginning and it was not up to us to decide anything on our own. We rushed through the meadow, wrecked the grass, and finally were again at the place we knew already, the for-real training ground.

We climbed down and got our ammunition and our orders, what we should do and what we should not. Already we were up again and holding on to our monsters by the teeth and claws. They were to fan out and, as soon as we jumped off and lay down, open fire over us. No banging just for its own sake. Real fire with live ammo. And suddenly up front a green rocket flew. Far up in front by the target, soldiers climbed out of the trenches by twos and threes, and everywhere, instead of whispers and the fire of the weapons, you could hear voices. It must look that way when an armistice is proclaimed. We climbed down again—no one had any objections to that—and we began to light our first morning cigarettes. Someone who had brought bread started eating it, and the officers disappeared. But soon they were all back again: they carried their helmets in their hands and scratched their sweaty heads, looking out of character.

We crowded around them, but one of them still was in the mood to bawl us out so we had to form ranks. The officers were debating among themselves as to who would make the announcement. They picked one officer, one fatter than was proper for an officer, and he told us in a squeaky voice that the commander of the regiment had ordered a change of exercise. The fellows shouted a hurrah, for each felt that the new assignment would not be a hornet's nest, and the squeaky captain reddened, but waited until we were quiet. Only then did he go on saying that joking was out of place, for it was a matter of life or death. That's right, you could hear from the guys, but the captain began to shout about what sort of rabble we were and we should watch out or they would prolong the drill, it won't happen every time that children go and get lost in order to spare us a proper maneuver. So we hushed and looked at one another: what children was he talking about?

The squadron commanders drew out their maps and divided the zones of assignment. All trifles made of metal or leather we had already shed and left by the tanks. We made a long chain and set out at a partridge beaters' slow pace, to find a four-year-old boy from the village last seen hard by the boundary of the off-limits area. He had got lost the morning before, and it was said that there was a suspicion that he had strayed somewhere in the woods, on the hillsides among their fallen trees, in some shot-up ruin of a village, or on the deserted roads of a gigantically enlarged Battle of Lipany under the broad sky—all this for grown-ups not yet grown up.

The Festival
by the Lake

☆

That evening they shot off fireworks, and the colored rockets revealed boats on the lake's surface and the shadows of their seated figures. Otherwise one could see only yellow paper lanterns on the water and the gray wedges of a few small sailing boats. The pine trees and the hills on the opposite side were limned very weakly against the dark sky.

In the wooded arena near the shore a comedian was entertaining the crowd, and each time he finished a joke, the band would start up a march to accompany the applause. There was dancing in a small shanty among the trees. The bar was full of soldiers and faces with raised chins and eyebrows, so they could see through the open door and onto the dance floor. On the road along the bank crowds gathered here and there.

On the benches people sat close together, and the glow of the fireworks lit up their candid snapshots. An officer with glazed eyes pressed toward a frightened woman and squeezed her hand in his lap. Through the crowd slipped a man with a sleeping child in his arms. The young men shouted: "We want beer!" A volunteer nurse in a white apron swayed through the surf of steps. She reached a drunken man sitting on the wall by the path, raised his head by the drooping hair, examined his face with its partly opened, lifeless mouth, and dropped it again.

A voice from a loudspeaker wove swiftly and drunkenly among the trees: "Miss Anička Straková should come to the local broadcasting station. Soldiers from Turnov are waiting for her." Insulted and neglected, there stood among the pine trees in the darkness a dark, painted combine. People were always coming near where there were already crowds. Around a truck full of barrels bent figures flocked together busily drinking in silence. Amid the crowd an acetylene torch shone up into the crowns of the pine trees.

It lasted late into the morning, and in the woods were left hats, cigarette boxes, the odor of vomit, and a few figures asleep with their legs pulled up toward their bellies. In the parking lot there were cars with heads sleeping on the steering wheels and buses with yellow lights by the ceiling.

The next morning there were boxing matches near the shore in the wooded arena. Young men on awkward legs gave way to their opponents, and when blows fell, the crowd on the benches among the trees shouted. The gong could be heard far out on the water, which under the rain clouds had turned green and was rippled by the strong wind, so that one could see whitecaps on the waves. The din drove the gulls high aloft above the straying boats and the tilting sailboats.

In the wooded arena the crowd stormed against the referees and was quieted only when they gave in and changed their verdict. Behind the arena, among the trees, there stood brand new shining autos on exhibit, and nearby beneath the tent of the puppet theater a loudspeaker roared: "At half past ten there will be the first presentation, edifying for the young and entertaining for the old." Acrobats and clowns practiced on the canvas gables of the tent. Opposite the lake shore a yellow glider lay tilted on its wing with a flag painted on its helm; from a truck they unloaded an airplane engine. Among the trees the loudspeakers cried emphatically: "Official announcement. Pilots, go at once to the vehicle line. Last car leaving for the airport."

Early in the afternoon a dark-gray plane flew over the lake and at the same time smoke rose from several small boats. From the middle of the lake a rose-colored smoke floated toward the northeastern corner. The plane altered its direction in an arc, flying in a straight line into the wind. A black dot came loose from the fuselage, flew in a free fall, and then over the dot there opened a white parachute.

The people on the bank raised their faces and tried to guess where it would fall. A motorboat with a flag sounded its horn and headed toward the path of the fall. The parachute inclined over the surface, moved over it a few dozen feet, and then deflated. You could see the head of a floating man. The pink smoke lay down and then thickened again.

The wind rose and the waves beat against the grassy bank of the lake, bound together by the roots of the pine trees. The plane came back over the lake, audibly gained speed and two more parachutes appeared in rapid succession. The children blew up balloons, and binoculars were raised toward the gray sky and followed the swinging bodies bound by ropes. The awkward oars of the rowboats splashed water. Men ran over the roots and sand to be near the place where the parachute would fall. A fat woman in a pink bathing cap bobbed lightly on the waves, as if her shoulders were made of cork.

The wind leaned against the pine trees, but they were strong and did not yield. A man with a pole on the side of the motorboat pulled the deflated wet parachutes out of the water. Each gust of the ever stronger wind carried a few bars of a polka. The plane came back again and along its fuselage two more parachutes appeared. The white combs and yellow rowboats furrowed the brownish-green lake.

"It will hit them," the faces raised toward the two parachutes said.

They had already crossed the bank and were quickly approaching the crowns of the pine trees. The legs of the hanging bodies were tensed forward. The people on the bank rushed into the trees after the chutes. In the woods the shade of the clouds was thicker than over the lake. The first parachute was wafted onto the last pine tree before the birch and pine copse. A man in overalls caught on a tree trunk and soon began to free himself from the ropes of the parachute, which hung from the crown of the tree. He cast off his spare chute and swimming vest and climbed up the tree to loosen the ropes. From the copse emerged a man in a shabby Sunday suit with one sleeve pinned up. He looked up.

"Is that Franta? Franta, where the hell are you climbing?"

"To catch squirrels," said the man in the treetop, kicking away the dry twigs, which got in the way of his work with the ropes.

"Who was jumping with you?" asked the man with the pinned-up sleeve.

"Kubiasová."

Down below, under the tree, people were looking up; and a couple spread out a blanket, lay down, and watched the futile work with the ropes. The man in overalls sat down on the twigs and combed his hair. He was trying to find where the ropes had gotten stuck.

On the far side of the copse a hill rose, grown over with tall pine trees. On one tree there hung a girl in overalls caught in the ropes. The gust of wind rocked her, and only the dry branch that pierced her side moderated the tossing of her body. Men ran back and forth below the tree.

"Go for a ladder," one called.

"A canvas, get a canvas right away. And you, nurse, where's the ambulance?"

The volunteer nurse in her white cape, white satchel at her side, walked heavily up the hill. Through the woods they were hauling an old firemen's ladder. They set it in place, but it reached only halfway to the top. The wind carried the bars of a march and the honking of the boat horns through the trees. People gazed up at the hanging girl, who by now had fainted.

"We need ropes."

"A canvas—cut it out and lower it from above."

"Do you know what a parachute costs?"

"Shut up. Get an ambulance."

Two men mounted the ladder and climbed on up toward the girl. They pulled her in toward the trunk and began to free the straps of the chute. She came to for a moment and then her head sank again. The two men were soon gleaming with sweat; below, the people were silent, with raised chins.

"Good God," the nurse cried and hurled herself toward the wheel of the firemen's ladder. The body of the girl in overalls disappeared into the cavity below the tree. The men on the tree stared fixedly downwards. The lower one looked at his bloodied arm, from which the girl had slipped.

The nurse raised gently by the hair the drooping head of the girl in overalls and looked into her face. Then she began to open the angular satchel, soiling it with her bloodied fingers.

"Where are they, the bastards," growled the man on the slope among the leaves of blueberries. "An ambulance, do you hear!?"

The band came closer with a few more bars in the wind. From the road along the lake people came in summer dresses and sportshirts, and asked what had happened, and they looked upwards to where, in the crown of the pine tree, the wind was tangling the white fabric of the parachute.

The Hands

☆

Jašek noticed it first. He was in the toilet, and through a knothole in the old gray wood he saw a red gleam. It was lower than our cottage, to the west of us below the bare slope of Plecháč. We rushed outside. It had rained in spells that day, but at night it cleared up, began to freeze, and the glasslike surface of the snow shone in the glow of the moon.

"It's the inn at Rezek," said Tichánek.

"It can't be—that's farther off," Kuneš asserted.

"Let's go, fellows," said Jašek, and we rushed back into the cottage.

There were four of us, and we lived in the attic at Schien's, who was a carpenter. It was a cottage by the woods, perhaps half a mile outside. In the valley below, the grass was already green in places. When we came back outside, dressed for the weather, with light narrow cross-country skis in our hands, old Schien stood in front of the cottage in his long underwear.

"It isn't worth it. Everything's finished already," he said.

We saw that the fire had grown stronger in the meantime and now cast a glow on the woods as if on a sea of waves. When we set our skis on the snow, they struck it like rock. That afternoon Tichánek had turned his ankle in the heavy, wet snow. There was bleeding, and now, at half past nine, his foot was swollen and had turned blue. Perhaps it was more than just a hemorrhage. We all took a look at it and resolved the next day to take him to a doctor. He had gotten dressed as quickly as we had and was now lowering the tip of his shoe into the binding of the ski.

"Tichánek, you'll only make it worse."

"Don't go, really."

"Nonsense," he said. "Look here." And he headed out ahead of all of us, down a bit and onto the road. Like the devil. Tichánek skied the best of us all and we were hard pressed to keep up with him. It was a wonder that he was able to put on his shoe. But when we had to go uphill a bit on the road near Vyhídka, it wasn't so hard to keep pace with him. His breathing was excellent and people said he had real Finnish form. Now, with his injury, we could keep up with him. The center of the fire disappeared behind the slope and all we could see was the glow in front of us. There was nothing in the clear sky to reflect the fire, and so it seemed as if it had devoured everything and was dying out. Through the corner of the forest that we had to pass, we could only follow other people's tracks. It was growing dark and we could hear only our regular breathing and the pounding of our skis against the hard crust of the snow. On the bare slope were four hurrying figures that the moon cast against the mirror of the frozen snow, bent far forward, overtaking their own weight. It was a longer trip than we had expected. Here on the open plain we could see how each step was agony for Tichánek. The decisive movement is in the ankle, which is made in a single second to transfer the whole weight of the body onto the toe. And at the same moment the body is hurried foreward into another step. It is a pressure from above downward. I caught up to him and rode alongside him.

"Ski home slowly and go to bed," I told him.

"You go ahead, I'll catch up."

"Go home and don't be crazy," we cried back to him.

He slowed down his pace, but kept his tempo with his head bent forward, casting the long poles far in front and drawing himself onto them. He always looked good when he skied. I always wanted to equal him. Already he had won second-division matches three times, and he was suppose to ski next year in a first division match. Now that he was behind, I led the group. It pleased me to notice that Jašek and Kuneš had trouble keeping up with me when I spurted forward. The fire could be seen beyond the bend, but we had been mistaken. It wasn't Rezek. We could see people running about their huts in the light from the windows. From somewhere far ahead we could hear the firemen's trumpet. It was a cottage at Stráž, and we had a good two more miles to reach it, either by going through the valley past Rezek, across the brook and up the hill again, or along the mountain through Plecháč. I headed up. I thought that would be quicker, since eventually we would be heading down a steep hill toward Stráž. We caught our second wind and were making good time in the freezing cold. Only the trail was furrowed here and our legs hurt. Then the fire reappeared below us. Figures flashed by in front of it. Outside there were cupboards, beds, and a couple of rearing horses. When we stopped in front of the decline for a second, we could hear the flames crackle and the dull thuds of falling beams. A man's voice was shouting: "Tanya, where are you? Tanya, where are you?" And a woman answered from somewhere: "Here, don't you make a disturbance." We descended in short arcs. They were taking the furniture out of the neighboring cottage. Its shingle roof was beginning to smoke from the sparks and they were afraid that it too would catch fire. Of the cottage itself only the two tall chimneys and the enclosing foundation block remained. From above it looked like a view of a burning boat, picked up on a high wave of the steep incline. A few people stood around indifferently or searched through the heaps of furniture, straw mattresses, and suitcases, looking for their things. The teeth of a child wrapped in a blanket chattered. We helped them carry out the furniture from the cottage next door. It took a long time and it was then after midnight, and when everything was finally out, we experienced a pleasant fatigue in our legs, backs, and arms. The fire still crackled and flared up here and there. Meanwhile the moon had disappeared. We had no taste for struggling up the steep slope of Plecháč, and took the way through the woods below with our skis on our shoulders. You couldn't see a single pace ahead. We walked slowly and in silence. We felt fine, thrashed as we were after a whole day and a night. To talk would have spoiled the charm. And what would we have said? Only at Rezek did we put our skis back on and advance the pace a bit when we began to feel the cold. It was after three in the morning and the temperature could have been as low as ten degrees above zero.

"Tichánek must be in bed," said Jašek.

On the ice our legs had grown stiff and begun to be awkward. Fifteen miles of travel at night were precisely calculated to equal a long, deep sleep. In the cottage we tiptoed up the stairs, but our desire to awake no one was in vain. The door to the attic space creaked horribly. We stopped short, as if we all realized suddenly that the darkness was quite empty. Kuneš bent over Tichánek's bed.

"Where could we have passed him?" said Jašek.

"At Plecháč. On the way back we were coasting downhill."

We collected sugar and chocolate and set off. It was beginning to dawn with a greenish light. We felt fear too in our legs. The snow was frozen to a dead, bonelike crust. What good was Finnish form now?

But we put into it everything we had left. He was lying there on the path on the slope, a hundred yards from the declivity toward the hut in Stráž. In short light knickers, he had no gloves on his whitened hands and was bareheaded. He was still limber. His heart could scarcely be heard. We placed him on four of our skis and carefully crunched downhill to the burned-out hut. There they were bringing the furniture back into the neighboring hut. They thronged around us and we had to drive them off. A doctor was there who examined him.

"Quick, his hands. See how? Rub his hands briskly with snow."

First we had to penetrate beneath the hard crust. And even then it was sharp, hard icy snow. Tichánek came to and groaned with pain. The sun was coming up and we could feel the choking breath of the dead fire. The furniture we had carried out that night was now all inside again.

The Bathroom with the Silver Faucets

They stood in the vestibule. The bargirl, dressed in a black jacket with white satin lapels, was speaking to a little bald man.

"Please, Mr. Böhm, do something for Alice."

Alice was wearing a long flowered dress, mostly green, pulled quite far beneath the shoulder. She looked unfriendly.

"I'll help you, girlie," Mr. Böhm said. "There's Krakow here. Can you take that?"

"How much?" said Alice

"We must be sensible."

"I have enough time to get sense—when I lose my voice. How much?"

"Alice," the bargirl said, "Mr. Böhm means well by you."

"He does and he doesn't. He doesn't know much, and none of those other girls has my kind of range. Which of them can take maracas in hand? Just you tell me. I could have sung at the Starbar in Vienna.

Does any of them know German *and* Italian *and* Spanish? I can sing anything, no matter what the lingo. And I don't need a mike stuck in my mouth the way those gals do, with their whiskey voices. Krakow, you say—well, how much?

In the swinging door a violinist appeared. He had a rounded back and part of his sunken chest was covered by his handkerchief, which was tucked under his collar.

"My dear lady, be so kind," he said.

Alice let her gaze pass slowly from his feet to his comically respectful face. She jumped up quickly, and two steps into the ballroom permitted her to transform her persona. Into the dim reddish light, full of tables, glasses, and people, there stepped the Mistress of Ceremonies, who was giving out fleeting but obliging smiles. She inclined the microphone to her lips.

"In response to your general wish," she announced, "we will play and sing Dr. Dušan Palka's favorite song: 'The World Doesn't Care for Tears.'"

The guests hummed the slow melody along with her and when it was finished some of them applauded. Most of the racket, made to sound like applause, was put up by the drummer.

"And now the latest Italian tango, 'Bambino mio.'"

She finished and left the podium. Her smile withdrew as she came nearer to the exit.

A man in a tux, the bass player in the five-member orchestra, sat on the rail that surrounded the podium from behind:

"For that kind of *bedelibiori* they pay her a hundred more every evening. That's Italian? For that let her put silver faucets in her bathtub and sing to herself in the tub."

He bent over the "preluding" pianist.

"Do, re, mi, fa, sol, la . . . . Well, so you've heard her. *Bederioli tamtamore bambino mio*, for a hundred crowns an evening extra. Off key, in a whisper, as if she wanted to gobble up that microphone, and there she is. I knew Anna Marie Bezoušková. Later she called herself Anne Spies, they liked it better in Moscow if she was German, and she knew her stuff in German—no *bederioli*. She sang in that diplomatic bar. It was a great number and they paid her well. No nickels and dimes were good enough for her."

"So let's get going," said the violinist, swinging his bow alongside the violin.

"We've got time enough, O.K.? Let them rest a while, how about it? I should fetch her? Doesn't she know herself when she's going to go on?"

The bass player crossed the ballroom and opened the door to the anteroom. The wardrobe lady looked over the counter and licked her lips. A man who had just come out of the men's room buttoned his fly and stopped, out of curiosity. Mr. Böhm bent his head down to Alice Farkašová's wrist and kissed it. The bargirl winked at Alice.

"So please do something for Mr. Böhm, Alice," she said.

"How much?" asked Alice and slowly lit up a

brave smile as if she were in front of the microphone.

"Don't worry, it'll be a lot, Alice," whispered Mr.
Böhm."

"When does it start?"

"Right away. Tomorrow, maybe."

"A bit slower. Be sensible, fellow."

She waved her scarf at him and went into the ballroom. The bass player trudged after her. She
grabbed the microphone.

"And now to please you all: Alan Svetlík's foxtrot,
'Not Everyone Knows His Happiness at Once.'"

An Evening at the Store

"Jesus, what's that again—such firing," said the saleswoman. There was light only inside the store; people came in from the street where the lights had gone out. They stopped at the counter and spoke across it to the saleswoman. The salvos came, like the people, through the wide-open door, but they could also be heard from the light, from the glassed-in compartments behind the counter, from the bottles, cans, cardboard boxes. Everything shook a bit, and in the intervals between the firing it went silent again. At the cashier's desk a man sat with head drooping; he did not look at the customers as they paid, but only made change for them from a dish on the counter or with paper money from a drawer. He turned around to the saleswoman, who was frightened by the shots.

"Miládka," he said.

Another salvo covered his whispering.

"Couldn't they stop it—why all this nonsense?" the saleswoman said.

"Miládka," said the man at the cashier's desk. "Be quiet. It's the October Revolution."

"October!" she said. "Why, it's November now."

He clinked five coins together, gave out a receipt, and again turned to her.

"They'll fire you and then nobody will want you anywhere. In Russia they used to have October as late as early November. And stop talking before somebody hears you."

More salvos came through the gaping doorway. The street became more noisy, but now with something other than the din of streetcars or cars. It was the shuffle of steps in the semidarkness. People overflowed from the sidewalks into the middle of the street. In front of the lined-up cars a policeman stood, near the illuminated entrance, and he could be heard speaking to a man who had just gotten out of the car in front of him.

"You've got to yield to the community. I've got my orders; you can't drive through."

The green neon sign on the house opposite was blending with the people's faces. The saleswoman had no customers for a time and looked out through the door.

"I didn't know you were so clever," she said. "Anyway, why do you talk to me? But you've heard it from me now: Either you come with me tomorrow or I won't stay here another minute."

"Miládka," said the man at the cashier's desk.

"Look, they're coming for me now," and she pointed with her chin.

"What will they do with you?" said the manager,

bending over as he spread out the money in the drawer.

"You'll see what," she said and turned to the two men.

Already they were indicating what they wanted with their hands. But before they could speak, she spoke to them.

"Just a second, I'll get my coat."

"Miládka," the manager called to her. "Wait on these gentlemen!"

She didn't reply. She came back in an overcoat, partly made up. She went through the door beside the cashier's desk and spoke to the two customers.

"We can go now, gentlemen."

Confused, they looked at one another. Fresh salvos entered the store on the paving-stones and clambered up the shelves toward the ceiling and then back down again. The manager got up and tried to reach for Miládka, who was standing near him. She turned to him before he could touch her.

"Don't touch me."

He stretched out his arm and knocked over the dish with the coins. They rolled far and wide over the paving stones. Miládka didn't pay any attention to them.

"Shall we go?" she turned to the two men.

One of them bent over and picked up the money. Circling in a squat position he wiped the damp, dirty floor with his coat. The other shook his head and looked up, as if he were waiting for it to stop raining. Then slowly he entered the dark stream with the green surface, full of heads. The salvos mixed with the shuffle of steps and penetrated to the inside.

Miládka stood among the spilled coins with the two men, one a customer, and the manager in a white apron squatting and doing a dance. There were only three or four ten-haler pieces left. The manager looked up at Miládka.

"Get back at the counter or it's all over!" he said in a low voice. And to the customer, who had placed a handful of coins in his palm, he added in a full voice, "You're very kind. What can I do for you?"

"Nothing," said Miládka. "We're off together to see the fireworks, isn't that so, sir? So long. Long live the October Revolution."

She offered her arm so the customer could take it in his. The salvos made the glass clatter, then fell to the floor and died.

"You have a fine salesgirl here, manager," said the customer. "I'll come again some other time," and he raised his hat to Miládka.

He soon disappeared down the street. The lights there were going on, the cars started their engines, the roadway was cleared, and half-empty streetcars started off. The policemen yielded to the cars and the salvos finished. The manager returned to the cashier's desk and sat down. Miládka bent over toward him.

"So how is it with us? Are you coming with me tomorrow to see the Viennese comedian, or would you rather play the perfect husband at home?"

A Wedding in Town

I've known him a long time. You can't call us friends, but when we do meet, we always have plenty to talk about. We never make appointments, but it does happen that we run into each other. At that time they hadn't requisitioned the YMCA yet for allegedly serious purposes. He came there to the gallery all heated up, even though it was wintertime. A white silk scarf hung round his neck, his winter coat was thrown lightly over his shoulders, and while still standing on the top stair he took it off.

"How are you, Tubbie?" he greeted me and walked slowly up to me. But judging by his use of that old nickname, I could tell at once that everything was all right, that he was anticipating something pleasant, or was amused by something, or that he had enough money in his pocket.

"Hi, Whirlie," I said to him, since his name was Whirler and that was what we called him. "Sit down."

He kept his scarf on. His face was a glowing red. That was the way one's face always looked after coming from the swimming pool at the YMCA.

And he was notorious for spending so much time in the steam room. He liked the sauna as well, with its dry air. But first he always did a hundred, two hundred meters in the transparent, greenish water above the white tiles and green lines on the bottom. These were always twisting, turning, and then straightening out again. The best time to swim was early in the afternoon, before the crowd came. And it wasn't half past two yet. He looked satisfied, and when he sat down, he cautiously pulled up his dark, nearly black trousers.

"What are you celebrating?" I asked, because it was a work day, early in the afternoon, and he was wearing holiday attire.

"My brother and I are going to a wedding," he said. "Our sister's getting married. Mila, you know her. Just try to think, you must have seen her sometime."

"Yes, I've met her," I said, although I recalled nothing. So it was Sister Mila.

"She's marrying Horna. You know him too, he used to be a sprinter for Slavie. But a yellow-bellied chicken as a runner, under eleven seconds just once in his whole life. You remember him. Good Lord, those were the days—we used to go there to watch them run."

He loosened his scarf and glanced down over the rail. Horna, Horna, I didn't quite remember. But I did recall Slavie. A dark sports dais in a state of repair, looking toward the west. There was almost no room for standees, only papers and half-broken pottery mugs, because on Sunday at the soccer games people stood on them to be higher. Behind the goal was a red-blue signboard, divided horizontally, with Fernet as a goalkeeper. Everything had gotten bogged down and no one was scoring any records. Only now and then in the shotput, high jump, or in long-distance running, but I never had any luck at that. Racing was difficult, because the track was a rectangle with four sharp turns, not those gently curving ones.

Whirler looked down at the clock planted on the large, empty, yellow-gray wall. Through the large, tall windows one could look out onto the wet street. In the morning snow had fallen and now it was thawing. I had stopped in for a coffee and would have left by then, but now I didn't wish to clear out right away.

"It couldn't stop now," he said, and continued looking down.

"We'll still get some more," I told him.

"You think so?"

"You can bet on it."

He ordered coffee, but since the waiter was already heading back toward his little room where the bell rang whenever the dumbwaiter came up with food, he called him back.

"What are you drinking?" he asked me.

"You can decide, if you're paying."

"Wait a minute. I didn't say I'd pay. We'll play for it," and he started to get up. "Two cognacs, waiter, filled right up."

"As you wish, Doctor," smiled the thin, short little man in the gray vest.

"And why aren't you wearing your favorite tailcoat?" said Whirler after him as he went slowly to the wall for a cue stick.

"We've all had our wings clipped—isn't that right, Doctor?" the waiter answered him, frowning with his sunken cheeks, and disappeared into the little room.

"Since when are you a doctor?" I said when we were already by the wall and were trying out cues. I liked the one that was quite heavy and had an undulating black end, which gave the fingers something solid to grasp.

"For him, always. But how can we call him a swallow now, when his wings have been clipped?"

He glanced with one eye closed along the length of the cue, then set its heavy end on the floor and began to apply chalk. He brushed the blue dust off his lapel and slowly bent over the green table. He was testing how the smooth wood ran through his bent fingers. No balls had been put down as yet. He looked about at the counting frame on the wall with its black, yellow, and red rings. Using his cue, he pushed them to one side.

"What handicap do you want?" he asked.

"How much'll you give?"

"Fifteen. No more than that today. Last time you wiped me out with twenty."

"You must be mixing me up with somebody

else," I told him. It could have been a year since we last played together.

"That doesn't matter. You've got fifteen and you can start."

I counted fifteen on my scoring frame, while the waiter gracefully rolled out two yellowish-white balls and one pretty red one on the table. They sparkled when he turned on the three lightbulbs in a tin shade hanging quite low over the green canvas.

Whirler glanced over the railing at the clock on the large yellow-gray, empty wall. It was in the middle, and its large hands jumped every two minutes, quivered a bit, and settled down.

"Is that clock right?" he asked. "What time have you got?"

"I don't have a watch."

"Waiter, what time is it—but the right time, please," he called, leaning a little bit toward the door.

"What would you like, Doctor?" the waiter looked out of his little room.

"What time is it?"

"It's precisely . . ." the waiter looked toward a small pocket near the belt of his black trousers. "Precisely twenty minutes to three. You can count on it, Doctor. Greenwich Mean Time."

"What's that?"

"Greenwich, if you please. It's on the meridian."

"Good, good. But where are those cognacs, learned gentleman?"

"They're coming, Doctor." He turned around and disappeared.

"Your turn, Tubbie. He promised to pick me up by two-thirty. You begin."

I hadn't played for a long time. The last time was with Petr Hojer. Not at that table, at the one beside it. He tried to escape and they caught him. Now he's in the Jáchymov mines. He gave me a handicap of fifty and scored one hundred twice. He lived in Vysočany on Krocínka Street. Once I spent the night there. In the morning his mother served me white coffee, more milk than coffee, and told me: "What do you think of our Petr? I'm sure he'll get into trouble some day." If you take the stairs down from his house and keep going down and then along a wall of white, faded bricks, you come out at Odkolek, a factory equally white. It smells there: it stinks of too-sweet cocoa. Then there were three train tracks and former barriers, of which there now remains only a single wood crossing for pedestrians. I hurried off to work and ran down those stairs. Beside the white wall I threw up from the running and the stench. Petr didn't go to work that day. That was the last time I saw him.

With luck and effort I scored a seven.

"So let's look at that more closely," said Whirler, drank half his glass, went around the billiard table to the opposite side, with his cue slightly raised in front of him he looked at the layout on the table, came back again to where he had stood before, took aim like lightning, and that was it. He had them all in a corner and knocked them away with fine jabs for a count of thirty-two. He stretched his limbs.

"Waiter, another cognac," he said loudly. He finished what was left in his glass. "Have you got anything against that, Tubbie?"

"Yes, I have. I can't afford it," I said.

"You don't say," he said and, stretched out over the whole table, he scored thirty-three points. The bright light fell on his colored, shining hair, pomaded while still damp. "It was payday yesterday, how could you be without?"

"What do you know about it?" I asked.

"You don't say," he kept walking around the table, always a bit bent over as he estimated the distance with squinting eyes. "How could you not have any? And where are you working now, anyway?"

"Do you want anything, Doctor?" the waiter said as he came close.

"Keep out of the way, it's just the right moment," said Whirler and lowered the fine leather end of the cue slantwise to the edge of a ball, so that they all snuggled into the corner like kittens in a basket. On the clock in the middle of the empty wall it was half past three when he made a sixty-three point carambole. That meant that it was really about quarter to four. We had each drunk our third glass. I could feel the warmth in my feet and I was in good spirits. He leaned back against the polished longer side of the table and wielded the cue from behind his back along the soft edge of the playing surface. When he gazed down his left arm at the ball, he had two chins. He felt fine. He had taken the day off and gotten ready for the wedding. The white scarf was hanging around his neck now over his lapels. His cheeks were red again.

"Just wait," he said, and he threw the cue in a large arc to the front again and this time he wielded it leaning with his belly and stretched over one of the shorter sides of the table.

His white ball with the two fine dots gently knocked the red ball into the corner, and when it bounded back from the shorter edge and then from the opposite long one from the other short one, it then should have come back to the other white ball, which was waiting for it, quite close to the red ball. But instead it shuffled quite slowly already across the table. He "helped" it by moving his cue through the air, and the muscles on his neck even swelled a bit. He forced it on. When it lost velocity, it turned a bit to the side and stopped there, staying put by the rail.

"The swine, it isn't up to it," he said. He scored his sixty-three and came back to our table. "Your turn, sir."

I felt I was more adroit, but I wasn't. That was the cognac. A great deal of money was at stake now. He looked at me and then bent over the railing to glance at the clock.

"He'll get it!" he said. "But play, play, let's finish up." He lit a cigarette and looked out the large windows. Among the reflections of the lighted lamps of the coffee house, autos splashed in the wet, blue outdoors, and precisely here the street the cars began to brake before the crossing.

"Where does it take place?" I asked him and started around the table slowly, so as not to lose my balance. He had sixty-three and I twenty-five. Six glasses: that was a lot.

"In Písecká Street," he said.

"You could be there right away, that's no distance at all," I told him.

But he had nothing to say to this, and remained sitting on the edge of his chair, a little bent over, watching the billiard table.

"He'll really get it," he said and only said no to the waiter who picked up his tray and offered to bring another round.

I had scored thirty, and slowly I counted up point after point. The stairs to the gallery creaked, and up came a guest looking around in search of a place, but it wasn't Whirler's brother. I saw him straight in front of my cue, he had his head right over the table as if I were aiming into it. His head was veiled by a curtain of smoke. If I let him play, I thought, time would go faster for him. But I scored a point. Six cognacs was too much.

"No distance at all, you say," he only said.

"Twenty minutes—I used to live there. I know that street."

When you looked out of the window of that apartment to the left, you could see the chestnuts in the Olšany above the flower stands, over the wall and over the gravestones of the cemetery, which had their backs toward the street in indifference. On the fourth of May, before the uprising broke out, I was getting dressed there by the open window, so I could go out and see what was going on. Banners were coming into view; some German businesses were having their signs wiped off. Across the way a young girl came out onto the balcony. She had closely cropped hair like a boy might have when he hasn't been to a barber in three months. She bent over the railing and called: "Folks, can I come out now?" Someone pulled her back and slammed the balcony door behind her.

It was four o'clock when our score evened. He had just played again, but had miscued. He stood and chalked bright blue on the end of his cue. We could hear steps on the stairs. Beyond the railing a head appeared wrapped in fresh white material. It wasn't a veil, but a bandage. Whirler rested his cue against the table. Before I could catch it, it fell and struck the floor.

"Don't be foolish, Míra," he said and brought his brother to the table. They sat down and inclined their heads together. The white head gleamed: it was whiter than Whirler's scarf. I was standing on the other side of the billiard table, with the waiter beside me.

"And they really discharged you?" we could hear Whirler say.

"Why not?" said his brother. "I didn't do it. I was standing on the crossing and somebody hit me from behind. The snow hadn't melted yet. His car slid. And the collision pushed me into her full on."

Whirler glanced absentmindedly around the green table.

"How old was she?" he asked.

His brother shrugged his shoulders. With his palm he pointed to something a bit higher than the table.

"Something happened, didn't it?" said the waiter. He looked at me. Then he glanced at the light over the billiard table and asked: "May I turn out the light, please?"

☆ ☆
☆

☆

A Fateful Night

☆

☆ ☆

Yesterday evening V. from Žatec came with the news that in a suburb of that town a train had broken up a bus at a crossing. It was already dark. After the first stupefaction from the shock, screams had resounded. Then the first people approached the wreck. They helped those get up who were able to get up. They extricated and carried away the injured. There were few to help and they had no light. More people joined them from the vicinity, attracted by the shock, the cries, and the shouts. Night offered them their opportunity. None of them could be dazzled so easily with the chance to provide someone with the help that person required. Then there were also the dead lying about amid the destruction. And what profit is there in helping the dead? Each of them pursued his own ends. One began to undo the steering wheel of the bus. Another started to take out a glass pane that was still whole. Of use too were the storage battery, the leather from the seats, the speedometer, the lights, the suitcases and satchels. But these persons were cowards. The more heroic ventured to take the coats belonging to the unconscious and the dead. They snatched wallets from pockets, they unfastened wristwatches, took off shoes. It was night, and each of them was pursuing his dream. Before the firemen came with their searchlights, many had had an opportunity to come to serious terms with their destiny and to carry away material tokens of that meaningful, fateful night.

On a Visit to
a Musician

Before he guided us to Carthage along Aeneas and Purcell's highway, to Dido's feet, we ate bread and butter and sliced pickles and he, with his eyes on the plate, told us about his invalid mother. He had come home one evening and discovered her trying to kill herself with gas. His wife and child slept in that room and their lives too were threatened.

"I could have killed her," he added, and wiped his moustache.

Through the open window we could hear a muffled rumble from the printing shop across the way and, at times, the tinkling of a bell. He closed the window and drew the curtain. He put a record on the open dusty phonograph. He placed himself over us like a gardener. He sowed a bed full of strange flowers and was happy at their radiance.

"My peace of soul and I are bound to part," sang Kirsten Flagstad. Purcell accompanied her with the silver of long waves. They struck against the glass of the windows and mixed with the cigarette smoke.

From Life

Another outstanding screening. You have to be an employee of the state film trust or a close acquaintance of a senior employee to get to come here, to see mostly average celluloid productions. But this time it turned out to be worthwhile.

Before it grew dark, they talked about a cameraman who had committed suicide. Supposedly he had left a letter in which he accused two directors and one producer of causing his death. He had waited until his wife went off to a dance before turning on the gas. Someone asked the senior cameraman R. who was responsible for it.

"Who? There simply are too many of us," he replied.

The film was called *The Third Man*. In a Vienna full of ruined buildings, the soldiers of the four occupying armies, crimes, the Prater with its gigantic Russian ring, a gang of swindlers, murderers, and bankrupt lives. Their leader is Orson Welles. In the end he takes flight through the network of canals, clambers up, clings to a grill and you can see how he stick his fingers frantically through the grill into the night street. Convulsive laughter sounded from the darkness of the projection booth.

A Day of Nothing but Foreigners

At eleven in the morning I dropped in at the Slavie coffee house. My customary table was already beleaguered with conversation. Joska was just beginning to talk about the time he was walking down National Avenue with Kamil L. and caught sight of Seydl in the distance, the very Seydl who so recently had spent a fortnight in our once imperial capital. Because Seydl continually turned out thickly contoured color drawings of beetles, because just as continually he submitted proposals for checkered jacket covers for books, and because, though himself a tall, awkward person, he had married a small wife with strikingly short legs, the opinion spread about him was that he was an original. That judgment was so common, indeed, that it even influenced Kamil, whose views and verdicts were almost always independent. Now when Joska caught sight of the recently returned Seydl, he looked forward to all the gossip he might hear. Instead of greeting him properly he blurted out: "What's new?"

And he heard in reply: "Things are fine, fellows. Since childhood I haven't felt as happy as I was those two weeks. They aren't good painters there, but that's not it: people are so sincere, and how fond they are of us. Someone would ask me on the street, where am I from, and when I told him, he'd pick me up and show me off to all the people standing about: 'Look here, a Czechoslovak.' My God, the traffic! I do know some big cities, after all, but they're nothing to write home about. And galleries, they're full of people for days on end. If you want to see the best pictures, you've got to have connections. And they'd always ask us: 'You're from Czechoslovakia? How, please, do you make those turning-lathes of yours?' It's all indescribable."

"So long," they told him and walked on.

"Idiot. But maybe he isn't as stupid as he makes himself out to be," Joska finished his story and hurried off to his office three buildings to the east.

Almost at the same moment Jan arrived. He was going off to Romania. He had a scholarship.

"Take DDT with you," Jiří advised him, "and sprinkle it all over yourself, especially under the armpits. It's a rough land. You can see things there. How about our one philosopher—do you ever get a chance to talk to him?"

And I added my own question: "Does he still claim Soviet Communism is a steamroller and it isn't going to adapt to us; we must adapt to it?"

"You don't understand him," Jan said. "That's

only a pose, which internally doesn't mean anything.
It's like when you go somewhere where they call you
'comrade.' You end up calling them that too . . . "

"It depends."

"But he decided at a certain point that he would
call them that and be sincere about it. Philosophical-
ly he hasn't changed in the slightest."

"But where is there anything that could change?"
murmured Jiří. "He hasn't managed to get out a decent book. He's had enough time to do it, too."

"That isn't his fault."

"Whose fault is it—can you tell me that?"

"There are many factors involved in it. All his con-
temporaries have managed that sort of thing, in their
families, at university, in their publicity. But not him.
His wife's a shrew. And he's totally impractical."

And another Jiří, a scenario writer wearing a
bowtie and with an open book in his hand, called to
me from another table.

"Please, help me with this sentence."

It was something in English. About one of the
Bills, fabled heroes of the American frontier in trudg-
ing on toward the West.

"'He looked and fear came over him suddenly.'"
Some sentences in a foreign language seem signifi-
cant at first glance but then yield nothing.

"Thanks," the scenario writer Jiří said. "And keep
nagging me about that Eliot—one of these days I'll
really give it back to you."

He had kept my translation of *The Family Re-*

union for at least a year. The way things stand no theater here plans to stage it for the present; although it could serve—in this country—as a gentle critique of the powers that be. Or would they connect it with Lord Acton and his remark that power corrupts and absolute power corrupts absolutely? Assuming that the authorities here know him—they don't seem to.

So the whole day concerned things foreign, especially when, to top it off, at three in the afternoon the telephone rang and it was a widowed Mrs. Müller saying that her son, another Jiří, had left a package for me before departing. I thought she was being too cautious since what she meant was that she had gotten something for me again from Jiří in London. In the package I would find Bartok's Piano Concerto with Monika Haas and God knows what else. I had asked my prewar friend Jirka—now Jiří Müller, employed by Ascher in Wigmore Street, with an apartment in Hampstead, a veteran of the RAF who came to Prague two months ago to bury his father and then wanted to know what I would like to have—for that concerto. His father was likely one of the very finest men we had here. In his youth a legionnaire in Russia, after his return ten years later head of a firm for importing and exporting foodstuffs and wines for the Controkomise: the legionnaires flocked about him to find some reward for their merits, when the great majority of others neglected to reward them. What I saw and heard at the age of seventeen—a very sensitive age—inside an apartment over the

vaults of the Pštros Winecellar, was the English saying that "Business is a nasty business," a swindle,
applied only minimally under Müller. This was as
evident to others as it was to me. Only I was put off
a bit by the oval, colorfully painted placard that told
one that Karel Müller was honorary consul of the
Republic of Guatemala. The banana and coffee
plantations along the isthmus joining the two Ameri-
cas were, according to my information, shoring up
anything but models of democratic or socially just
societies. I once ventured to point this out.

"And when you were five," the consul graciously
addressed me with the intimate pronoun as he
would have his own son, and this was an honor,
"were you already so clever that such things mat-
tered to you? *They* are less than five, and if they
didn't have enough customers, their people would
perish every day in numbers far greater than they do
now, so that none of them would ever grow up."

"Daddy," his real son Jiří called from the window
where he was adroitly stringing a tennis racket, "why
don't you go into Parliament? I might even vote for
you when I'm grown up."

"You and your friends are too much for me," Mr.
Müller said somewhat distractedly and then absentmindedly, with his back to the two of us as he himself prepared to go into his study in the next room.

It was then the Year of Our Lord 1935 or 1936. I
had the chance to appreciate his murmured, amused
melancholy only three years later, when things got

started. Yes, all three of them—father, mother, and
son—escaped in time, but so many other sons,
mothers, fathers, were left behind. After the catastrophe the father and mother, still courageous, returned
to the street called Pštros. Through his service to the
RAF the son had not only gained British citizenship,
but a certain kind of wisdom that warned him to
avoid further adventures: this time in his own country, without an open war, and with persons not
elected but of a special stamp who were in power,
though not through parliamentary means. He would
fly to Prague only occasionally, when the powers-
that-be gave him permission.

"My fate is that of a father," Father Müller said to
me at intermission time during the weak soccer year
of 1954 at Sparta Stadium. Jirka guessed that better
than I did.

I don't know anymore if I was able to tell him that
clearly enough, but the idea was that his poorer
guessing did him honor. No doubt he stayed here
out of a feeling of solidarity with his local club,
which was for the most part made up of legionnaires, of Jews, of pilots wearing royal insignia, of
people thinking in a humane way, thoughtlessly divided. Even at that final meeting Father Müller addressed me in the intimate singular. This time he
meant it as brother to brother, and so again it was an
honor that was even flattering. Two and a half years
after the war there appeared the newspaper, *The National Liberation*, a daily that was quintessentially le-

gionnaire. In 1945 the twelve members of the editorial board took me on, still a boy, as one of their number. And so legionnaire Müller was to have a chance to read something of mine from time to time. Up until February 1948, that is. And now he was telling me on the platform at Sparta that I had known almost the same thing as Jirka, only he said that I knew how to write about it. Especially that weak human proclivity for the avalanche: Where twenty idiots go, they are at once followed by a million idiots still more stupid, and the worst thing is that among the total number of idiots, intelligence plays the main role as the outstanding servant of the candidates for the motes and beams of power. But, people ask: Why doesn't Masaryk's humanism spread like an avalanche?

Does anybody know the answer? Does our only remaining philosopher know it, at least peripherally?

On my way to Wenceslaus Square I bought some carnations for Mrs. Müller because even there, in the middle of the metropolis, which is on the way to the most human arrangement for all things, they didn't have anything better or even different. We now have a new order, one in which people obviously don't buy flowers on Saturday; hence the leftovers wither away over the weekend and our centralized economic planning suffers. The emptiness of the stalls made me think of a fireworks display I once saw, of colors and forms and faces, set off early in the morning in a stormy but pleasing fashion for two blocks in front of the flower shop onto the sidewalks of the Parisian boulevards, in the direction of the Boulevard St. Michel.

The Parisians are evidently duped by that multi-colored magnificence so that they forget their countless unbearable wrongs and ornament their dwelling places, lapels, and declarations of love with the tinsel of flowers. Only, which duped person tends these effusions of delicately proffered and extremely simple beauty so that they should appear on the sidewalk just at the right time? Can he really be a deceived simpleton? The servant of an empty stall in the broad sunlight of the promised and just order rather looks like such a person. As a matter of fact, the centralized planning system is badly mistaken in the matter of the public's interest in flowers on Saturdays. Before the bored flower seller can tie up his sold merchandise, four potential customers have come and gone. A gentle young girl, no doubt in search of a gift for Mama, says only "Oh yes" and skips along. A lady, nicely got up and scented, of Mme. Bovary's years, is seeking an adornment for an evening *a deux*, and when she spots those wrinkled flowers of Revolution, she is unable to restrain herself: "We got just what we deserved." An elderly gentleman has presumably thought to sacrifice half his pension for a nice Saturday with a lady friend from times long past. He looks to have been raised a true Victorian, but when he sees the supply, he blurts out, "Shit!" And the same thing was repeated a minute later by a young dandy, who got out of his car, kicked one of the supports of the stall and drove off again in his polished coupe.

In the inherited apartment on Pštros Street, which they had renamed a while back in any case, the rooms were chilly without carpets, the furniture was pushed into the corners, and in the foyer the feather mattresses stood propped against the walls. The plucky little surviving widow led me inside; on the late director's desk lay a stout, gray parcel.

"Don't get angry at us," she said, "it's only a trifle. And I have some phonograph records here, if you'd like them. Masaryk's speech from 1928."

Obviously I couldn't refuse. She wrapped up the records. All the work had fallen on her, she said, and she was moving to London to join her son. She promised to phone me once more before leaving.

I hurried away. It was a lot of work tying the parcel onto my motorcycle. At home we opened it and there were used shirts, undershorts, and a suit worn by the late consul. It had become a fact that not only do one's relatives have poor relations, but friends too have poor friends. This was, in a certain sense, a discovery. None of the Müllers had ever really looked poor, but you could see they were.

We played Masaryk on the phonograph. At the beginning, during his speech to the young people, the children make a great deal of noise, which Bartok might have found suitable had he written another Concerto for Orchestra. At times you could hear the great Prospero, somewhat overshadowed, quiet the children with a single word.

"Greetings."

As is evident not only from the continuation of his speech, he was using this word in accord with an old traditional custom. In that foreign land of long ago, politicians and statesmen did greet people so. They did not give orders telling where and how people were to be greeted.

Things Help Life but Also Death

An old house with a heavy swinging gate that yields to the hand. A corridor with cellar smells: potatoes, coal, a vague damp. On the walls, spots. Well-tramped stairs, in the middle of a rising curve a tiny cross on the wall fastened with a sprig of heather or something. To the right of the staircase, a brown door with a handle that looked as if it were bent down with fatigue, worn out with walking, smoothed out with touching. It is already loose in its doorjamb: it clinks and rattles, shakes and hisses whenever there's a strong draft. A thousand times people have commented that something will happen to it. Outside there is a spring wind at the sunset hour. Here sunset comes early, the street is narrow, the house's front facade points toward the north, the windows of the entrance open into the narrow court to the east. The door of the apartment opens to the outside; with a turn of the handle and a turn back again, one enters. The door gives out a sound of age-old desolation. It was as if this machine for opening up human dwelling places, this austere, manifest fruit of civilization had become nature again, and with some kind of vegetative will had taken up the idea of imitating its age-old fellows. But it is imprisoned and fettered. Feeling the cold, it clicks jaw against jaw. Inside, a small dark anteroom. On its right side, a door to a bedroom. There you find dusk and deadness. The door on the left is amazingly white, smooth with its chromium handle. Repairs have been made here. The house's venerability has yielded here, someone has ventured to try to surmount it. To carve in a cavern, hollowed out in the atmosphere of the end of the last century, a niche that at least resembles the bright, restrained, impersonally neat "apartment-house" culture of today.

Behind this white door a suicide has taken place. They were a young couple; together they had sought to introduce these innovations. After a year of this he told her he had chosen badly, but it was just such things that bound her more tightly to him. Even the daily journey through the odor from the cellar and the decrepitude of the staircase that led up to the new white door and on beyond it, to that which was a consecration of their union. He had acted honorably, he claimed, he had told her everything, he asked for a divorce. That spring evening she took luminal and turned on the gas.

The Happy Summer

They owned a factory for agriculture machinery. But their yard was overgrown with grass, and through the door to the workshops you could see that nobody went there. Only in the storeroom three men were sitting and drinking beer. They had been kept on as long as possible, since they were old and had worked there from the time the business was founded. The company also had a residence house beside the railway station in Rozvaly, with a long veranda at one end from which you could see the shunting locomotives, the semaphores, and the hard gleam of the rails.

The old factory owner had died and his son had inherited the debt-encumbered enterprise. No one wanted new threshing machines or plows, and the factory grew deserted. The young owner had a wife who wore her hair close to the head, divided at the part. Their nephew, who spent his summers with them, was called Martin.

There were wicker chairs on the veranda, and from the veranda's corner the booming of the phonograph opened up a strident world. Records were thrown about on the table. *La Paloma,* Mozart's *Eine kleine Nachtmusik*. Martin played them, then he stood by the open window on the veranda and the sun was as hot as a warm showerbath when the cold tap is turned off. The iron rattle of the rails beneath the passing express blended with Mozart in the warm torrent of summer.

One day his aunt came, raised the needle from the record and shut the window.

"In case a storm comes up, you know. Come in and change your clothes, we're going somewhere."

Uncle owned a green American car with a large nickel searchlight on the left side of the rear window. They got in and seated Martin between them. It was as pleasant as the window on the veranda, with Mozart, the sun, and the locomotives. His aunt warmed him and seemed springy. They drove through the warm dust of the highway.

"I'll take the Mozart—that's for sure," Aunt said.

"Take what you like—only shut up about it, please."

Uncle was rather small and had to raise his chin over the steering wheel. Mozart was dropped, and there remained only the pleasant warm sun, drying the greenery of the trees along the highway. Martin felt like huddling so that he would not touch either one of them.

"I won't go back with you," said Aunt. "I'll stay with Lola. And you'll send my things after me."

"Just as you wish. Only be quiet."

Martin inclined his head and did not look at the dusty trees that were passing. He had the feeling that the next day he would have to go to a cold school with corridors painted green and with black toilets, smelling of fresh tar.

On the square in Kolín, Uncle stopped. Aunt stroked Martin, but he would not look up. When they both had got out, Martin spent a whole half hour moving the gearshift from side to side and not looking out. He could detect the perfume from his aunt. If he were to look up, he would not have held back. His uncle got in, banged the door shut, and drove off. They were crossing the bridge to Zálabí.

His uncle kept an easel at home and sometimes painted. In the cozy room behind drawn shutters you could smell the paints and the turpentine. On the wall small paintings hung in dark-brown, red, and orange colors. They showed people in a coffee house. But everywhere on the paintings there was only dark-brown gloom, and out of that emerged a single table with a light over it and three or four people sitting around it. All the women had hair like Aunt and the men looked like Uncle, with his raised chin and slightly closed eyes. It seemed as if Uncle carried something within himself but did not know how to speak about it. It looked out from his eyes like those small bulbs shining into the room's obscurity. He had learned to paint from the artist Kolert. And now they were going to his villa in Zálabí.

They left Martin in the studio and went to the livingroom alongside it. By the wall, beneath the slanting window stood a canvas of a donkey amid the dried-up, stony Italian landscape. Martin sat down in front of it, but the donkey was not alive. He felt an empty and dead painting. Martin went over to the sofa and placed himself on it with his head down. He was thinking of his aunt, of how she had turned off the music and shut the window.

When they were together, Uncle and Aunt, it was summer. When Uncle was alone, it was the end of summer.

In the evening he ate with his uncle in the restaurant on the main square. Martin didn't look to see whether it resembled Uncle's paintings. He didn't raise his eyes from his plate. Only once did he look at his uncle, to find that there was much more of that which his uncle didn't understand, but about which he would have liked to speak.

The waiter came, bent over toward Uncle and then led him off to the telephone. When Uncle returned, he didn't sit down again and they drove off. Dusk was beginning and Martin strained his eyesight.

"Aunt!" he cried.

She was standing on the edge of the sidewalk and waving for them to stop. She got in and placed Martin on her lap. He feared he might be too heavy for her, but then during the ride he put his head on her shoulder and felt her warm face on his forehead. He closed his eyes and felt wonderful. He was submerged in her warmth as in the window by the station and the music. They supposed he was asleep.

"You must think it over as soon as possible. He'll endorse our loan, but I have to be nice to him," said Aunt.

"So you actually had a chance to talk to him?"

"He came to see Lola."

"And you're really taking it seriously?"

"You can be glad about it, can't you? And anyway, I like him."

"You're—" said Uncle and swallowed something.

"You knew what sort of woman you were marrying."

Martin rocked on her lap in the uneven rhythm of the ride. The dark into which he sunk when he closed his eyes had a strange taste. It was coming from her, and he had the feeling that he should turn and embrace her around the neck, do something to make her be silent. When she talked, it wrung him as if he couldn't give an answer in school and had to stand at the blackboard. Whenever she was silent and was here pressing so close to him, soft and perfumed like the dark itself, streaming through the open windows, then it was evening with a cut-up apple beside his bed and the first shining lights of sleep.

"Don't think I'm going to let you drag me through a life of poverty. I didn't marry you for that. With your painting you don't earn enough to pay for your funeral."

Martin waited dolefully until her final word

sounded. It took too long. He twitched on her lap, turned and clasped her around the neck.

"What's wrong, Martin? Sleep."

And she stroked his hair. Slowly he settled down beside her, but he held her by the hand and every little while he gazed at her to see if she were asleep, for otherwise she would begin to talk again. Uncle raised his chin into the window on the veranda when the rails gleamed in the sunshine and behind him the music was playing.

On the Sky's
Clayey Bottom

She sits on the threshold of the house by the railway track, her hands with their withered, stretched fingers placed on her skinny thighs, which are covered with the pale material of an ancient dress with a floral pattern. Wrinkles around the mouth are pulled inward; the lips cannot be seen. She leans her head against the whitewashed wall; her hair is braided in a small knot. It is a warm noon with soft puffs of wind. The hurry of life vanishes in the distance, as the pair of hard, shining rails vanishes in the curve below the slope. There remains the wide, slowly rising hillside on the other side of the track, divided into long strips of fields. Through the doorway beside the old woman, as well as through the window, a band can be heard playing softly on the radio. A knife, held in someone's hand, is cutting and striking against a chopping board. Then the same hand moves the pots on the stove about; the gushing water hisses and crackles. Lower down, right by the track, a man stands in a dark uniform. A bell rings and the man goes to lock the gates, which lower slowly into their metal cradles. The dusty highway is empty. The old woman on the threshold is motionless. To the left, far off, there rises and comes nearer the black blossom of smoke. The wind carries a dull, muted noise.

"Then he would always prick up his ears, and I would hold him by the collar," the old woman thinks.

The black din of the freight train moves along the tracks before her. The man below by the gates stands straight with a red flag at his side. He salutes the engineer, and around the corner of the locomotive the engineer raises his dirty fingers to his forehead.

"That's how Haryk always used to want to run along the track," the woman thinks. "Sometimes I'd let him go. And then he'd come back and put his face in my lap. There's no lap left anymore. No one would put his head there."

"Mama, what is it—can't you hear?" a voice calls through the window.

"If only you'd shut up," thinks the woman on the threshold and remains motionless.

"Dinner, I mean," the voice calls from the window.

"You couldn't give him a child, so shut up," the woman thinks.

The gates rise slowly, they open to a draft of emptiness above the track and the man slowly climbs towards his dwelling. He stops alongside her.

"Didn't you hear? Let's go to dinner."

"Why didn't you find Haryk?" the woman on the threshold says.

"Mama, don't be angry and come. Or we'll have another row."

"You've taken everything away from me."

"So up, let's go," the man smiles at her and takes her gently by both elbows.

"You should have taken her like that and not left her to no purpose."

"Should I bring your soup out here, then?"

"You should have brought it for *her*. To her, and in a proper way. Not leave her like this."

"You know what happened."

"We're dead. Every day funerals come at us headlong. And you can't even find Haryk."

She is speaking into the void over the long gentle slope, over the railroad gates, which are rising. Empty poles without flying colors.

"We're all dead. Each day twenty funerals, back and forth, with a noisy funeral band in uniform. Sometimes some child behind the window raises a white hand and waves for the last time. It disappears behind the grave of the slope. Every day they will hold the funerals of some of their children. My grandsons and granddaughters. Haryk always ran out and greeted them. But he wouldn't even go look for Haryk. He never even came to her bed in the proper way. We are dead on the sky's clayey bottom. She'd never been warm enough. We're three dead people at the gate to the abyss. The child would see trains and faces through the windows. It would jump and look forward to Engineer Burda's coming by. He would always whistle at the children and thumb his nose at them. We could be living children and anticipate Burda's coming, the colors of the dresses outside the windows. Watch to see which kind of smoke comes from the eleven o'clock and which from the two o'clock express. Count the cars and imagine what they contain. But they never found the right moment, and we are three dead persons at the end of the abyss. And he couldn't find Haryk, either."

"Here it is, Mama. I'll hold it for you. Eat up, that's right."

"Why didn't you bring Haryk back?"

"It's four years now since he's gone, Mama. Eat up."

From the window another voice is heard.

"You're always being difficult. Can't you come inside, Mama? Something always seems to be bothering you."

The Afternoon
of a Faun

Early in the morning many people left the island. The season was over, and by afternoon the beach was empty. A motorboat pulled up sporting a machine-gun on the bow, and the shore police went swimming. At both its extremities the horseshoe of sand ended in a rocky declivity. We swam beneath a cliff where the transparent water came in among the rocks, foamed, and ran back again. It was tricky to keep your footing when the surf came in, to not be hurled onto the sharp rocks. During the night a hard, warm wind had been blowing, following a brief evening storm, and now the sea was replying belatedly, beneath the blazing sun. The police boat turned out and slowly diminished in size on the low horizon of the open sea. The smaller it became, the more its thin flagpole rocked. We swam for a long time. On the shore we lay down on the warm sand. Inside the misty gleaming space under our closed eyelids we were still.

We took our fill of the sun and slowly got up to leave. Tiho looked about the beach and saw no one.

"Let's go," he said. Everyone had left.

We followed the path up between the stony hillsides. The olive trees had turned gray and the tamarisks seemed to be weary of their continuous erect posture. As we climbed up to the highest part of the island, the plane of the sea, visible among the trees along the path, broadened into the great distance.

In the shade of the trees Tiho asked, "Where's my blue girl?"

He stopped at the edge of the path, his face to the hillside, and roared with all his might.

He turned toward me quickly. "That German girl, did you see her? And how! I'm going to have her!"

He turned back toward the hillside, where a cricket chirped in the dry tufts of grass. He yodeled. He began to shake his head slowly as we climbed on up.

"Where's my blue girl? She's in Zagreb. No, she isn't yet, but tomorrow she will be. In Zagreb."

He took me by the arm. "We agreed on it. Next year we're going on a trip around the Mediterranean. For 50,000 dinars. You must come too. This morning I turned out two drawings. They came out fine. You must take a long look at them. With the German girl there's nothing but sex. I'm going to have her. And how about the Czech girl, the red commissar? You'll keep me up to date. But she's too cold. I don't like red commissars who're cold. She looks that way, too. Isn't it true? My blue one, where's she now?"

He raised his chin and yodeled again at the horizon. "I'm glad I met up with you here. I'll learn English. I'm taking courses in Belgrade. Now I'm working up to the intermediate level. I already know a thousand words and by next year I'll know six thousand. But I like French girls better. I'll have that German girl, you'll see. I've already put up three houses. I like colors: one is pink, the second green, the third blue. You have to see my drawings. Two blocks from the harbor, the Hotel Pracat."

We were climbing down from the island's crest toward the harbor. The sun's reflection from the sea kept hitting our eyes. He stopped and sniffed the dry grass by the path.

Finally he shouted, "I've got to have her! Let's go. And next year you'll come with us, on the *Yugoslavia*. Have you seen her? For 50,000. And we'll talk English together. We'll go with that blue girl of mine."

By the Grand Hotel it was sultry and quiet. In the arbor of orange trees an elderly lady was sitting by a table reading. Other guests were beginning to emerge from the dark lobby of the hotel. Tiho remained standing and looked up toward the terrace on the third floor. He shook his head and sat down at a table. We ordered coffee, but on the other side of the hedge he caught sight of a green table and ran to the concierge for paddles and a ball.

"Let's play ping-pong!"

He thrust one paddle into my hand and we headed toward the table.

"I'll beat you—you'll see! I'm a whiz!"

Quickly he set his arms and legs in motion. Every so often he turned toward the terrace on the third floor. He pointed with his paddle.

"They're staying there. And the drawings, we musn't forget them. You'll like them. We'll go have some rakia and I'll bring them. When you sit outside the tavern you can hear the fishermen telling stories, and the sea. I must come every year. Let's play."

I won very few points except during the moments when he was looking at the terrace. He exulted at each winning point. It was humid and we were sweating. He shouted all the more, the more his face glowed.

"I know how this game is played! I'm going to beat you! Like this . . . see? Twenty-one, hurrah! Let's have another game!"

He put the ball in play, but suddenly laid down his paddle.

"Just a minute!" he said. "I'll be right back. Or don't wait for me. In the evening we'll meet in front of the tavern. I'll bring the drawings and I'll draw you my houses."

He went into the hotel lobby. The sun was already low in the sky and into it was sailing the white police boat with the raised barrel of the machine-gun on the bow. It was already far out on the open sea, and the boat rocked on the waves raised by yesterday's storm.

Tomorrow Begins

The only communication with the mainland was at half-past five in the morning. Women with baskets on their laps and children by their knees were already sitting on the boat. An old man was leaning with his forehead on his stick and catching up on lost sleep. The boat's motion rocked him as the men jumped from the stone jetty into the aisle between the benches, or onto the roof of the cabin, and loaded on boxes and baskets. They talked rapidly and loudly into the morning wind; the sun shone aslant over the olive trees and tamarisks on the hillside beyond the embankment. The town was little more than the embankment and a row of houses. To the east the semicircle was completed by the steeple of a church. It was reflected in the quite peaceful surface outside the harbor jetty as it undulated. By a quarter to six the boat was full of people, boxes, and baskets of wine. I found a place only on the open stern. Beside me sat a skinny woman in a flowered dress who kept firing off an uninterrupted series of sounds to an old woman on the jetty. Beside the old woman there stood a man with thick, wide lips. He was leaning with his hands on his knees and bowing to the woman in the boat. She was sitting with her back to him, and her browned face on her long, aging neck turned to him with its sharp projecting nose. She had reddish hair, and pulled up her hands into the sleeves of her overcoat. From time to time the man on the jetty smoothed back his thin hair. At times he squinted, gazing along the embankment toward the hotel. The embankment was empty and in the shade. The man spoke school English and the woman the same. She threw in German words when she needed them.

"Tell your wife I couldn't help it," she said.

"Don't mention it. Why do you mention it?" the man said.

"Mr. Glavović said yesterday that the weather would turn bad for two or three days, but that then it would be fine," the woman said. "Take advantage of it. You'll still have a wonderful vacation. Mr. Glavović has lived here on the island for thirty years. I didn't realize he used to be the owner of the Grand. Did you know that, Olga?"

She had turned to a girl who wore a blue cape with puffed sleeves sitting beside her. The blue girl shook her head. Her hair was blonde and at times she shivered with cold. Her neighbor, a young man with a moustache, ran his arm along her shoulder.

"It must be a terrible thing to own a hotel and then own nothing. How can he support himself now?" The redhaired woman went on. "Give my best to the beach. I won't go swimming there any more, not till next year. Next year—maybe. Your wife is angry at me—."

"You lost the feeling," the man said. "You had it for a while, but now you don't."

"It's so cold," she said and fussed with her hair. "Why isn't it warm all year long? In Zagreb it's going to be cold."

"I'll come on the tenth of October. I will never forget you."

Olga, the blue girl, drew her legs close together. Her neighbor with the moustache was whispering something to her. The old man woke up, extended his gray unshaven face, and with his stick tapped at the girl's back, which was bent over the edge of the boat and the water. She turned around to identify the guilty one. Everybody laughed and tried to out-shout the others. The red-haired woman in the flow-ered dress called out to the boat captain. She took me by the hand, looked at her watch, and went on talking even more vivaciously. On the roof of the cabin the captain threw up his hands and pointed to a house on the embankment.

"We'll miss our ship," said the red-haired woman. "Have we got all our things, Olga? She's not with it. Oh, I forgot to leave something for the maid. Be good and give her—"

She bent over to her purse.

"I'll take care of it," the man said.

"But no, you shouldn't. We may never come again. Where is my change purse?"

"Please, don't go on looking. Now it will be so lonely here. I'll feel completely alone. Promise me—"

"Here it is. Give her this. Please be so kind. When does the boat sail from Gruža? You don't know? Olga, do you know?"

"At half-past eight," said the young man with the moustache.

"And you're traveling with us, Mr. Tomíc? I'm so glad. We won't feel so strange on the ship. And Olga will certainly be pleased. Olga?"

"I'm not going yet. I leave on the eighth."

"On the eighth? You're a lucky man. What will Olga do?"

"Will you remember me from time to time?" the man said from the jetty. "I never adored anyone so much. Give me your hand—they've untied the boat already."

"Lopud! When will I see Lopud again?"

She extended her hand and looked toward the bank, the church, and the fortress on high.

"You'll still have it fine here, and your wife—"

"Dagmar, I never lo—"

"But they're not leaving! They're waiting for Mr. Randulić with the mail. Oh, the post office! And the church and the Šipan across the street. And the Grand, with its arbor of orange trees and the boys with guitars in the evening. They won't play today: it's Monday, they have the day off. Your wife played so beautifully on the piano the other day. Tell her—"

"I'll write you. I must meet you, on the tenth in Zagreb."

"Zagreb! It will be cold there, and there's no sea. Why can't there be sea everywhere?"

In the boat the engine rumbled and a malodorous smoke rose aloft at the stern. The little girl started to jump about and the old man dozed again, the boat swayed when the last passenger jumped aboard—a young man in a blue and white striped polo shirt underneath a sport jacket. He sat down on one of the boxes and the captain started to chase him away. There was a great deal of laughter and shouting. The captain leapt from the roof forward to the helm. The boat slowly broke away from the jetty. The man on the jetty straightened up.

"Have a good trip," he said.

He turned to walk away through several waving figures, heading toward the embankment.

"Don't forget the maid. And tell your wife—Olga, we're leaving Lopud, what do you think of that?" And then the red-haired woman passed over to the natural stream of her mother tongue.

The boat was small and avoided the open sea. It navigated close to the northern promontory with the chapel; on the other side, across the strait, the high, rising shore of the mainland was visible.

Relātā Referō

Sometimes the chit-chat came first hand, sometimes second hand, sometimes tenth hand. They repeated it to shorten the day, for their own fleeting fame, for a bit of excitement, something more like life than pounding a typewriter, gaping out the window, and the assigned reading of bureaucratic nonsense. In the office there stood a bottle of French wine and around it four glasses, each one different, cups for coffee, and the long, drawn-out afternoon lesson. The talk twisted about like heads following a flying shadow.

Their guide was a Jewish woman, ugly as night, but wonderfully likable. On the streets of that metropolis they saw poor people: how they carried bread home and, in a damp sack, cabbage. Not just one or two poor people. Whole processions. And some were from villages fifty miles away. They asked their guide how that could be. They have come to buy the city's cabbage, she told them. But how about bread—don't they have that at home? They want white bread, baked here in the great city. And to entertain them, she told them how it was when geese were exported to the metropolis by their Western neighbors. Everyone wanted to get them. She herself lived in a fifteen-room apartment. All by herself? they asked her. Oh, no, she laughed. It's fun because forty-five people live there. We have just one kitchen, one toilet, one bathroom. But everyone has a different shift, everyone works in a different place at a different time. It's all such fun for us. When the geese came from the West, we called meetings. A plan was worked out as to who could join the line and when. People waited from early evening till morning. It was fun to stand in the lines. Some people played harmonicas, some drank vodka, others sang or told stories. Life in a big city is rich and varied. And at last we got four Western geese. We arranged a business meeting and worked out a plan. Geese must be roasted as soon as they are bought, laughed the guide.

That makes sense. It's the same at the Opera House. A certain Dr. Bauer sings there. In *The Bartered Bride* he always sings the Circus Manager and his wife sings Esmerelda. He never speaks about it, but she has told me that. They own a villa, and that was a case for you. Not far from there lived a parquet-layer. He had three children, but he came into money so he bought new furniture while the kids got the upstairs room. They were looking forward to sleeping up there. He didn't want to let them because the paint hadn't dried yet, but the kids talked him into it. They had a stove in their room, but something happened to it, a fire started and the children burned up, since the parquet-layer and his wife slept downstairs and didn't hear anything until it was too late. They wanted to kill themselves, but Dr. Bauer talked them out of it, and so they went to live with him. The parquet-layer kept saying that he was eating the doctor out of house and home and that he should compensate him in some way. The doctor maintained that he shouldn't even mention it. But the parquet-layer said that he must do something, and he set out to polish all the floors in the whole villa. He mixed a large quantity of wax and carried it, still hot, into the first room. He tried to press the door-handle with his elbow and his lighted cigarette fell into the wax. It caught fire. He was so upset he didn't know what he was doing and set the burning tin down on the sofa. The Bauer grandfather, who also lived in the house, now came on the run. He seized the tin and tried to carry it out, but only succeeded in pouring it all over himself. His clothes caught fire and he died later in the hospital. Soon the whole room was on fire. Now when Dr. Bauer comes to give a school exam, they call him the fiery manager.

You all know Mr. Gerstel, the one with the hearing aid in his ear, how he's always mixing something up with his battery in his breast pocket. You know him, of course, old, balding, always talking about something. He'll grab you and talk your ear off. But he's got a wife too, and she must have been a beauty once. And she gets herself up. She's got a brother in America, and he sends her everything she needs. Her clothes are marvelous, but they don't seem to have enough money. Mr. Gerstel says they've sold everything, they've got only the bedroom left. He does the shopping and cooks himself, he does everything because he says: women, they belong in bed. That's it, and why do I say it? In Prague there were some real geese. Mr. Gerstel bought one. But when it was baked they couldn't eat it—it smelled of fish. He wrapped it up, put the fat in a jar, and took it all to the Ministry of Food. Just smell this, he said to the appropriate bureaucrat. You can't eat that. Why not? said the bureaucrat. You don't smell anything? Mr. Gerstel insisted. Nothing at all, the bureaucrat affirmed. Then you don't belong in the Ministry of Food, said Mr. Gerstel. It smells of fish and I'll have to buy another one. And he got one. His wife didn't even know that it was a different goose. He does everything himself and she spends the whole time in bed.

Those geese have to be roasted just right so that each person can have his share just when he gets hungry. When he comes home from his shift to rest, take a nap, and then head off again. The geese resisted, they were tough customers. They must have gotten old before they left the West. And so it didn't work out right. A goose always finished roasting at the wrong time, just when those who had already eaten one were still around, There were fights, but they were caused by the geese. If it weren't for the fact that they were tough, those forty-five people in the fifteen rooms wouldn't have known that there was any hatred or malice among them. It was the geese. For a long time we couldn't forget about them, the guide laughed. But that can hardly be the happiest sort of life, to be with so many people all the time, someone observed. You don't think so? the likable guide responded. And she broke into laughter that rather resembled tears. No one could cheer her up. She escaped from them, and the following day instead of her they had a male guide, a reserved young man with a severe forehead. They asked about her and he said, what was her name? I don't know her.

Come and take a look, do you see that shed there on the hill, it all happened near to that. There was a soldier. He came for some children on the playground and said he could teach them different games. They say he quite fascinated them. But still, most of the children were afraid of him and ran away. Only one young fellow stayed with him and let him take him over the hillside. And they found him only the next day, in the evening, because he lived with a stepmother but often visited his grandmother, and both of them thought he was at the other's house. He was stabbed terribly, but the doctor said that he lived some hours longer and died only toward morning.

They were a sight to see at the party. At the buffet each one took a different piece on his plate, placed himself in the middle of the hall, and fed others from his own plate. Like two turtle doves when they bill and coo. The director, nearly bald already, and his assistant, you know him: well washed, curly-haired, with a bowtie. But when the French theater was here, the director, for the sake of one of their actors, went with them all the way to Bratislava. What must his assistant have said to that? But they very likely take it quite differently. Each of them is happy that the other one has a success with somebody. Or do you think it's only an act?

When they got their new guide, they took the Metro and it was crammed full. They got on and had nowhere to sit. They called their new guide a police spy. He looked at three elderly women in kerchiefs and made a slight movement of his hand to indicate that they must get up. He left his arm lowered but moved his fingers at his side. Perhaps everyone there had learned to know their superiors by their faces, for the police spy wore no badge. They got up immediately. But no one wanted to sit down, it was terribly embarrassing. The whole car scowled at the scene. But God knows why. Were they offended that the foreigners were contemptuous of their hospitality in freeing up the seats? Or were they angry at both the police spy and the foreigners? And as they got out, the spy said to the people on the Metro: Remember, these are our guests.

They figured out what had happened terribly late. He had a cleaning woman who came everyday to his studio around the corner from us. When she came for the third time and it was still locked , she went to the security police but they told her, you know what artists are like. Then she went to his apartment, but he wasn't there either. So she called the janitor and they opened the studio. He was lying there with the gas turned on. He had puttied up all the cracks, so that it wouldn't get out. And he was naked—they say you die faster that way. He left a note, and they say he had written that the new bigwig was guilty, that when he was here last year he had called a monument the artist designed a scandal. They were supposed to pay him money for it, but they didn't give him anything. And everyone was rude to him. And he received anonymous letters in which they called him a pig, and asked how could he disfigure Prague that way? And they said his note finished like this: My wife, whom I had left, showed me the way. She had killed herself with gas a year earlier.

Perhaps you never heard how that big German shepherd dog died. The bigshots thought they could use it for propaganda and that maybe it would even bring in hard currency. They proposed to every country in the world that they make a monument to the dog, so that anyone who wanted to could bow to it. No one wanted to do that; only in Israel did the government meet and decide that it might double the amount of tourism if the german shepherd statue were put up just beside the Tomb of the Lord. So they sent off a telegram: Crate it up, send it off; we'll set it up, we'll pay for it. But when the whole corps of big shots got together and opened it, they couldn't bring themselves to decide. Suddenly one of them got up and said: Let's not do it, I wouldn't recommend that. There's been one resurrection here from the dead already.

The tourists were also invited to the homes of actors and writers. None of them had more than two rooms in his apartment. The largest apartment belonged to a senior puppeteer: three rooms. He had made the space look larger by pasting whole walls over with photo enlargements of Renaissance facades and colonnades in perspective. Only out of town, in their dachas, did they have luxury. One evening they visited a war novelist, and when they were leaving, he asked them where they would go that evening. They were invited to visit an elderly actor. The novelist went along with them. Right off, in the front doorway they could see that the actor was displeased. And he even referred to it as he talked. We don't visit one another here, he said. Each of us has two or three friends, and that's enough. Our Citizen Writer here can testify that he's never visited me before. They talked on and drank more, but he took it up again: He can testify to it himself that we prefer to be together in twos and threes. Now we won't see each other again for whole years on end. Isn't that true, Writer?

The Twelfth Mission

"If there is any salvation, it is in inactivity."
—J.M., former RAF navigator

Langford Court
London NW 4
September 1947

Dear Sir:

You ask me how it was with Vilda Kotas, with his heroism and his end. They told you I was the person who would know these matters best. Evidently they themselves wished to avoid answering. But it's just possible that I really do know the answer best. Whether this actually would be suitable for your Archive of Resistance—how can I say? But all right, since you need it for your archive, you shall have it. Vilda would no doubt get angry at me for wasting time instead of taking more interest in my wife, say; she is sitting here beside me mending stockings for our boy (he too is named Vilda, after *him*), and she is actually taking your part, for she has already told me several times: "Write to them how it happened, perhaps it will dawn on them, when you write how it really was, and they will realize that there must someday be an end to all that heroism." I believe that myself. Heroism is actually a terribly unpleasant thing. Especially when a person doesn't want to have anything to do with it himself, but someone else compels him to. It isn't nice to swallow salt water or feel how things beneath you are sinking slowly, and nothing can be done about it; all around only smoke flies from the burning engine; you look out to see if by chance some ship isn't going past, a ship which in actual fact never goes by, or if they haven't placed an island right there opposite, there where so far no one has ever discovered one. I was an idiot for ever getting involved, and if anything was worth all that dripping sweat, drifting at sea, or praying to the Lord God, for whom it was all a matter of indifference, then it was just my meeting with Vilda. Because although he too didn't know what was going to happen to him in this world, he didn't run around like all the others acting as if he did. I will tell you, then, what you wish to know, but whether it is suitable for the Archive of Resistance, I really don't know. Vilda was some ten or twelve years older than me. Today when I sit thinking about this, it strikes me how little I know about him, as far as his past goes. Where he was born, when precisely, and so forth. But I have the impression from the words that he scattered—

not that there were very many of them—that he was always successful in life, even though he never had to scramble to get ahead. Under the Republic he worked as a freight inspector, but that didn't interest him for very long. He did that about a year after the time of his discharge from the army. He still didn't escape promotion in the end—but I am getting ahead of the story. In short, he was headed elsewhere. First of all, apparently, to France, because he had met Exupéry somewhere. "There are as many good pilots as there are pilots," he said, when mention was made of Exupéry, "so why make a fuss about it?" From the very beginning I thought that Vilda's modesty was a bit put on, since everyone said of him that he was a pilot of the sort everyone should be. I don't know much about it myself—I was a navigator. And a navigator goes along for the ride, curses the pilot for not holding to the course, but still has to rely on that pilot because if he doesn't, he'll wind up in a coffin. Even when it turned out the way it finally did, with Vilda there certainly wasn't any obstacle to feeling oneself quite safe. But that wasn't due to his false modesty—there actually was no modesty. He simply supposed that other people had the very same value as he did. Otherwise he praised Exupéry, except that I do remember one time when he smiled slowly and said: "I'm curious to know if he won't get those aristocratic hands of his dirty." I didn't quite understand it at the time, but I know enough to know that he didn't intend it ironically. You would have had to hear the way he said it. I don't remember that he ever made fun of anybody, although people might think that he did, and often did think so. That was a common misunderstanding among people. He kept many things to himself, and that irritated people. Like those words about aristocratic hands. I understood it only much later, when I no longer had a chance to speak to him because he was no longer alive. But I'm getting ahead of the story again. My meeting with Vilda was amusing. They had sent us then to Bermuda, and along with us a band of fellows from every possible nation. It was the spring of 1941. Before they drafted us or before we enlisted, most of us were employed in factories in London and the industrial cities. You know, it was after the great air raids, and that awakened in us a longing to throw onto the heads of others the sort of thing that had fallen on us. We thought too that it would somehow bring the end quicker if we would just get in it. People always suppose they are important until they find out what things are really like. We didn't think they would send us so far away, and it irritated us a bit that we wouldn't be here when things really lit up the way they were going to; but that was only our mood, and the plans of war did with us whatever they wished. It was rumored that the real bombardment of Germany would begin very soon and we—or at least they told us this—we, along with a small number of experienced pilots and crews would constitute that first wave that would set things going on a large scale. So when we departed for the isles of paradise, where at any other time we would have longed to go, we kept looking backward. Ideas are always more tempting than the reality, and for the time being we could only imagine what an airfield was, operation meetings, preparations for flight take-off and flight itself, straight into hell. But at that time we didn't speak about hell. It all looked like glory. Most of us already had at least a part of the theory behind us, some had two or three hours of training flights, but otherwise we were "dreamy-eyed small fry," as Šimon Kouba, an old captain who walked with a limp, put it. He had a long record as a commercial pilot in the Czechoslovak Republic, but his leg had been crushed by a farmer's wagon. At least so he claimed. We three Czechs in the transport called him our "mentor." It was curious how he changed when he got to Bermuda. For the whole sea voyage he had been the best superior we could have asked for. I won't say that his joviality didn't get on my nerves a bit when they told us that there were mines around us or that we hadn't cleared the submarine zone yet, and he'd always tell us, in his terrible English, "They can't sink you twice." He'd laugh frightfully at his joke and here or there one lad would laugh with him, perhaps from a sense of obligation. But on Bermuda he was different. He stopped laughing, drank heavily, and kept making excuses to us. That was all connected with Vilda already. The or-

ganization evidently wasn't functioning too well, because when we arrived there, one airfield was already
full up and the second was only then being built.
Bulldozers were driving there—they dug up the grass
with bushes and trees and behind them they were
laying the concrete for an airstrip. They worked
quickly, but even so it took two weeks before we
could walk smartly over that concrete in our shirts
and shorts accompanied by our "mentor" and the
commander of the airfield. What they had plowed
up a week ago had already grown back, not only
grass, but shoots of undergrowth, tobacco leaves,
and all sorts of things. There was nothing tall in the
vicinity, only in the distance there was the kind of
church you have in England: two towers without a
steeple and a narrow peak of roof between them.
Among the trees you could sense the existence of
further homes, but you couldn't see them. No matter
how a man whirled about there, nowhere could he
catch on to anything. You know, people from the
hinterland. It looked to us as if there was water
under that grass. But they imported their soda water
from America. So we were standing there on the
freshly made airfield, and because no one was exactly speaking to our souls and we weren't forced to
crawl there on our stomachs, as they sometimes
made us do all morning long, I got the feeling that
we were on some sort of raft, sailing God knows
how and where, that there was no war at all, and no
longer any other people. And all of a sudden, before

I could turn aside again, I saw our "mentor" and the commander of the airfield—a short, bald, slightly stout Englishman—walking a short distance ahead of us, but now no longer alone. There were three others with them. I was a bit surprised: where could they have come from? "Look at them," Karel Ermler said to me—Karel, the one with whom I had left Czechoslovakia in '39 and who then right off on his first flight in a Mosquito was hit in the spine by shrapnel; he lived, but to this day he still can't walk. "Where could they have come from?" Obviously I wasn't the only one who thought they could have fallen from the moon. But they stood there and they clearly were fine fellows. All of them with their legs spread so slightly, with their hands in their trouser pockets, their blouses unbuttoned. Like somewhere at a garden party or a game of golf. Of course they didn't wear caps. They were heading toward us. We were curious, we welcomed every change—in people, in the weather, in our food, and most of all in the news reports. There was the radio and there was the *Hamilton Gazette*, but they were all too straight-laced. We wanted to hear what prospects we had of getting into it and where. The weeks ran on and they crammed into us nothing but theory. We wanted to have the feeling that we were really accomplishing something; we wanted to count off the hours as they flew by: how many of them were left before they would let us get in it. Two of them were dark-haired, their hair combed faultlessly. One of the two had a

fine, long scar stretching from one corner of his
mouth in the direction of his eye. Their hair must
have been pomaded, since it didn't stir in the wind.
The third was taller than the others but he was a bit
hunched in the shoulders, rather thin, and he didn't
withdraw his hands from his pockets as the other
two did when they stopped in front of us. He had
rather short blonde hair, the wind played with it on
his forehead, and he had a lean, narrow face and
slow, inquiring, contemplatively seeking eyes. It was
Vilda. He stayed a bit to the back while the other
two began to speak. We supposed then that something enormous had taken place. It struck all of us,
and we crowded close around them in a circle. We
didn't even pay much attention to Vilda, because he
had not yet spoken. We learned that it would start
the next day. The training planes were already in
Hamilton at the docks, they explained. They had
brought them from Canada; they themselves were
from there. I recall how one of them, a bearded Englishman with narrow shoulders, the kind we Czechs
call boyish, cried out in excitement and begged us to
sing their 'For he's a jolly good fellow', nonsense,
but we wanted to learn more about what was going
on—when America would get in it, what they had
done with Hess and such things—and so we were
busy outshouting one another with all sorts of talk,
but of song there was nothing. I must have exchanged a few words with Karel in Czech because
Vilda, with a totally unmilitary considerateness,

made his way over to us and quietly greeted us. I can't tell you any more how he did it. It was self-assured, without joviality, without sentimentality. He stood then in that pack next to us, listened to what the Canadians were saying, and said nothing until we were on the way back to our barracks. He stayed a bit behind the others, and in the end I fell back beside him myself, because Karel at that time was getting more nervous, terribly impatient, and needed to talk constantly. I bore his silence well on the whole, even when it occurred to me that this newcomer would liberate me from an awkward position since he was an officer, after all, and I hardly more than a young boy. He probably guessed what I was thinking, because he soon asked me when we had sailed away from England, and he inquired after several acquaintances of his, asking whether I knew anything about them. That was the way it always began. That personal world came together, dispersed over the whole impersonal world of seas, cities, airfields, continents. I knew nothing about any of the persons he mentioned. "Those two have a lot of experience behind them," he made a pointing gesture forward with his chin, indicating the two Canadians with whom he had come. "They'll know how to advise you. But what I'm doing here, God alone knows. So many people all in the same place." It looked as though he had been here alone for a long time and only now had found someone to whom he could voice his thoughts out loud. It was his good luck that

he had found me for this; with others such behavior
would most likely have undercut his authority. From
the very beginning he intrigued me. I don't recall
anymore how I replied to what he said, but we always, when we had time off, walked from the barracks to the canteen and back so that we invariably
ran into one another, even though we never made an
agreement to meet in advance. About ten days later
I had my first navigating lesson in actual flight. The
compass trembled in my hand, the figures kept
jumping in front of my eyes, and all the time I wanted to look at something firm outside the plane where
there were only waves, and the rocking, fogged-over
horizon. Vilda was checking the pilot and me. He
crawled from me to the pilot and back again. But he
struck me as somehow terribly absentminded. He
had it all in his little finger, he didn't have to think
about it very much. At one point I was quite off my
count. To use the flight time efficiently, they tested
for three or four different things on a single flight.
During the third I began to founder. My head
burned. I told myself I was a coward. I felt sick, and
besides, he kept looking at me over my shoulder. I
was all ready to throw in the towel, to tell the pilot to
head back home without instruments. And then perhaps Vilda realized, because all at once he leaned
over to me and said: "Don't worry—when you need
it, it'll come to you." He took the controls himself
and headed back to the field. We climbed out and
I said to him: "Yes, but I need it right now and I

haven't got it." Right after the flight we had to make a report, just as they made for real at the airfields in England. But here the authorities had plenty of time to investigate everything and make trouble for us. Later in England it was quite different. Whenever we got fed up with things we just turned our backs on them and left those officer journalists to think up something themselves. Here they questioned us at length. I was in a stupid position because I hadn't brought it off. Vilda took the notebook from my hand, told the pilot to get lost and not make his report just yet, until we called him, and we sat down in the grass underneath the wing of the plane. He opened the notebook and suddenly looked up. He had trained ears. Perhaps it was something even greater—he simply sensed what was in the air above. I saw him abruptly set the notebook with my calculations and my map aside and glance up toward the end of the runway. Another training jalopy was headed in from that direction. We saw it from the front. Slowly it grew larger, strangely, spasmodically, it rocked. It did not move straight forward, but kept slipping to the side. I was looking past Vilda, I saw how he gulped. He stretched his arm out in front of his face, as if he wanted to give the plane a warning. But the arm sank back again. And when that clumsy crow in front of us slid down along one wing, he was already up on his feet and running toward it. I went right after him. The fuselage had tilted forward on one side and it all had collapsed. Now it was only left to wait until it caught fire. A crowd of people ran out from the hangars. The ambulance was on its way. Vilda was the first to attempt to make his way inside. The others stayed in a respectful circle all around. One of the Canadians roared at Vilda not to lose his head, that it might still catch fire. When he saw that Vilda needed help, that he couldn't make his way in by himself, then he went in too. The school commander was already calling to us lads to keep back, so we couldn't do anything. They brought three bodies out. Some of the fellows had already seen similar things. For me it was a baptism. One of the men they brought out, the very one Vilda was carrying, suddenly made a strange movement with his arms, as if he were reaching for something in a bad dream. Vilda knelt down on one knee, set him slowly on the ground, unbuttoned his blouse, stroked him on the forehead, and then began to go through his own pockets. At that point I rushed up and handed him a pack of cigarettes because Vilda didn't have any of his own. It was old Kouba. He had merely lost consciousness. He looked past all our heads up to the sky and slowly exhaled smoke. "How are the others?" he asked. Vilda looked around. One ambulance was driving off and the other lurked nearby, to take the "mentor." The school commander, who was still calling to the other boys and the mechanics to keep back, made a sign to the ambulance. "How are the others?" asked Kouba, more loudly now, and raised himself on his elbow. "They're at peace from all this," said Vilda. Perhaps another man in his place would have thought up another phrase, one that would have postponed the news, or would have at least put it differently. I was irritated. They were dead no doubt, that was true, but still something of them lived on, their eagerness and ardor, their restless and un-satisfied anticipation. We felt it. It was going to live on as some sort of wild, wounded vitality in the rest of us—in me too. And Vilda had said they were at peace. We were all closely linked, and when one of us was hit, the shock went down the line, affecting us all. It wasn't fear, but tension rather, some sort of attempt to carry them along with ourselves, not to jettison them like carrion, to carry them further with us on our way to hell—that place that we thought of then as a fulfillment. And Vilda had said they were at peace. They carried Kouba away and we slowly went back to our calculations. The wind blew every-thing all over the place and I had to take awhile to gather it all together. I wasn't up to much then, and Vilda was called away to take part in the investiga-tion of the accident. I was left alone with it, and felt enraged at Vilda. I decided I didn't want to have anything to do with him. I thought that he was a show-off who only cared about his own security, that he didn't understand our task, didn't understand what the war was about. I avoided him. Kouba was given liberty, but he went on roaming about the camp, and I began to talk to him more often. He would bring up the accident at times, but only in a roundabout way. One evening we were standing in the canteen, listening to records sent us by some well-wisher on the staff. The bartender, whom we soon took to calling "Quaker," since when he had nothing to do he would walk back and forth behind the counter, whistle or mumble something and swing his arms in time to the music, came completely to life listening to those records. When I looked at him, it struck me as dangerous that we were beginning to feel too much at home here. His ruddy cheeks, the forelock of blond hair, the tiny blinking eyes, it was all too cozy; it recalled too much the pubkeepers, the tailors, the tobacconists—in a word, those merely half-recognized people of whom we are not even conscious when we resort to them in the towns of our homeland, but who, whenever we recollect them along the paths of war, remind us of the atmosphere of home. Kouba must have sensed this too, when we stood at the counter and Quaker kept turning his back on us to change the record. The "mentor" too most likely felt at home. And then that accident was still living in his mind. It was roughly ten days past. On the border of the airfield grass was beginning to grow over our first two crosses. He ordered a whiskey, which only officers were permitted to drink. It was about six o'clock in the evening. Through the windows, in which there was only netting, a warm air flowed. I was drinking beer. In Quaker's awkward hand the tone-arm fell on the record and the phonograph began to play "It Happened in Monterey," an old waltz I had heard at home when the boys from high school and I would go dancing Sunday afternoons. My throat tightened a bit. I took a long drink. The "mentor" said: "We'll dry up here just waiting. I don't like it. It takes too long to get something ready to make a proper start." I agreed. Two Englishmen came in from my barracks and stood alongside us. They stopped only to greet us with a civilian's raising of the hand, and then went on talking to each other. The two men killed in the training accident were also Englishmen. The "mentor" finished his drink in one gulp and asked for another. The waltz came to an end and, were it not for the conversation beside us, one could have heard only the breeze, the splash of whiskey flowing from the bottle into the glass and, somewhere in the distance, a muffled droning. "I'll explode from it all, Pavel," said the "mentor." "I haven't got nerves for it. Knowing they murder people there while we sit here." I answered that, after all, everyone does his share. Kouba waved his hand. "That's the sort of thing someone like Mr. Kotas thinks—he probably explained it to you that way," he nearly snapped. And then Kouba, the "mentor," revealed his secret to me. He had requested assignment to the bombing command before leaving England. But they had sent him here. He was too old for them. Immediately after the accident he repeated his request. And now he was waiting here, eating his heart out. I

rotated my glass on the bar and didn't know what to
tell him. "At least go back home once," leaped out of
me. "With all my troubles, that'd be a fine home-
coming. You're not talking now to Kotas—I've told
you that already." His irritability put me in a bad
temper. "What've you got against him?" I said. "He
climbed in there on your account." The "mentor"
laughed. "He'd have to climb into a lot of things for
me to believe him." The door squeaked and Vilda
came down the long aisle between the tables. On his
finger he was twirling some kind of key on a keyring.
I recall it so well because it was the last time I saw
him in Bermuda. For a year after that we didn't see
one another. The "mentor" had already drunk three
or four glasses earlier in the day. He made a movement as if to leave, then squeezed back against the
bar and asked for another drink. Vilda had now
reached us. "They've finally found out I'm no good
for morale," he said. "They're ordering me back." It
turned out later he was to serve as a test pilot for
planes on delivery. But at that time he didn't know it
yet. It was only clear that he was to go even farther
away from the war, which he had in fact been coming closer to during his stay in Bermuda. "To Canada?" Kouba asked. Vilda nodded and was evidently
a little puzzled at Kouba's glance. "And is that what
you want?" "How can we want or not want things?"
Vilda threw his hands into the air. Kouba spat in
front of him and said he was through with him.
Vilda only bent his head. That's how I remember

him best, with his head bent, with his high forehead looking ahead, incapable of formulating for others what he was capable of living and experiencing. What could he have told Kouba, or me? I have thought about it a great deal ever since, but then the war was still going on. Šimon Kouba died on a ship that hit a mine. I learned that only after the war was over. You must have some information about his death. I was assigned to the coastal command. We flew reconnoitering missions to search out submarines and patrol for convoys. As long as we were in training school, we were always together, as if we were guarding one another. We differed in our speech, our curses, our ranks, and our faces, but concerning that one thing that held us all together like a flock, we all expressed it in identically the same way: We cursed the Germans with contempt, our officers with annoyance, and we Czechs often argued whether our government in exile was worth anything or not. Then came the flights. That was something else. In that each of us had to be responsible for himself. The fellows changed. They became more serious, talked much less, their speech was formulated in hints and gestures. From the flights each had a similar experience, but also his own distinct ideas. It was time for them. But they were invariably kept hidden. Or they were expressed only after a few drinks. And the man who had to listen drank just as many drinks and followed his own train of thought or paid no heed at all. We were alone now, each one

of us alone, even though comradeship persisted. In
the coastal command especially there was loads of
free time. Some days we flew eight, ten, twelve hours
and saw nothing, only the sea down below, or the
clouds and sky up above. And then they got us. We
were flying over a convoy. The rear gunner saw
three fighter planes. It was an ambush, a thing we
had not encountered before. We landed on the
water. The gunner in the stern was dead, the pilot
wounded. I helped him out. In a minute the plane
was under water, and we were on a rubber raft. Toward evening a ship from the convoy took us
aboard. When, three weeks later, they asked me
where I would like to go, I thought of those terrible
hours of emptiness. I told them I would like to be
assigned to the bomber command. I thought it
would be over quicker that way. Without waiting
and without drifting. Without all the purgatory with
the map, the static on the intercom, or the
chronometer in front of the eyes. And in one week I
was there. In the command barracks they told me
that the wing commander would be back in a little
while. It was early morning, outside it was raining,
and they weren't going to be flying that night. It was
peaceful. I picked up the *Evening Standard* lying
there on a chair, probably an old issue, and I recall
that my gaze fell at once on a column from somewhere in the old world. It was about the king of mu-
sical comedy, Ivor Novello. He had bought gas on
the black market and they had arrested him. The

newspaper was briefly indignant, but it did not forget to print his handsome profile. I don't know how
I felt—half a year before I would have been annoyed
and would have expressed myself with a curse, but
now I looked at it all quite calmly. And I recalled
Vilda Kotas. Perhaps their faces were slightly similar—not much, because in my mind that would have
been unfair to Vilda. But in that newspaper there was
a sentence to the effect that Novello's month-long im-
prisonment in Wormwood Scrubs had brought the
harsh war to the remote confines of luxury and to a
fairy-tale world, created by him with his plays, his
melodies, and his play-acting. I sat there in the cold
of the office, the spectacled typist pounded on her
machine, two men bent over their desks, the walls
were hung with maps and documents amid perfectly
regular planks, outside the window it rained, from
time to time someone pushed the door open with his
foot, came in, laid something down on a desk and
again withdrew. I felt sleepy since I was dragging out
the last day of my leave. And then there was the dis-
cussion of two worlds in the paper. Just for that reason I recalled Vilda. Not because he had it any easier
anywhere outside the war, as that matinee idol had.
But he owned his own world. Can one reproach anyone for that? I asked. And the answer was—or is
now, at least—that we had given in to insanity, since
we identified our worlds with the world of someone
who knew how to get us in it. We accepted someone
else's arguments and put aside our own personal ob-

jections. Vilda Kotas did not accept these things, and
he remained overseas. Perhaps I did fall asleep there,
listening to the regular pounding of the typewriter.
Then the door flew open, someone knocked the
mud off his shoes, and two men crossed the room to
the door of the inner office. I got up slowly. The
smaller of the two was the wing commander. He
looked around and I took advantage of the fact to
announce my presence. He was gracious enough to
take three steps back toward me and shake my hand.
Slowly the other man turned too. It was Vilda Kotas.
He smiled and waited until the commander had
finished speaking. I learned that Vilda would command my aircraft. The commander went to his
office then and left us there. Vilda looked a good ten
years older than he had a year before, and his back
was even more hunched. I only said: "For God's
sake, are you here?" or something like that. I experienced more surprise than joy at this encounter. "The
old man can wait, let's go," he said and took me by
the arm. We went out into the rain. "Your name's
Pavel, is my memory correct?" he asked. "You were
with Kouba that time?" I nodded. Evidently he was
thinking of the scene in the canteen. For a while we
walked on in silence. We came to a row of bombers,
which stood there with their monstrous blunt noses
pointing toward the airfield and with their tails hidden underneath the trees. We stopped. "Do you
think it'll be over soon?" he asked me. But at once
he waved his hand and half turned away. "It's all the

same now, when it'll be over. All the same. Forgive me. All that's nonsense." And he asked me how I happened to get there. I told him. He only squeezed my shoulder, sent me to his quarters and promised to come back there to meet me. He had to see the commander. First I moved into my barracks and then I headed out in search of his quarters. He wasn't there yet, so I sat down on his bed. Some aviators decorated their rooms with pictures of their families or their girlfriends, with newspaper clippings or their own drawings, sometimes even with vases and various knick-knacks that, together with their laundry, no one knew what to do with when someone didn't return from a mission. Those aviators lived on in those trinkets and no one dared discard them. Only the maids from the housekeeping staff knew how to deal with them. For such things they had a basket and one room into which they gathered it all together. Besides what he had laid out or locked up in his wardrobe, Vilda had nothing in his room. Only the more impersonal parts of a toilet kit, and one ashtray. And he had been flying here for two months. He told me that when he came in. He was trying to drive away the gloomy impression he had made in me, as he supposed, in that earlier period. It was eleven in the morning and the weather was beginning to clear up. He talked of everything possible. How he had been furloughed to London for two weeks, but had turned right around and come back here. He felt more alone there than here, half asleep on his bed. He described certain people to me, people whom I later met. He told me about the Czechs who happened to come here and stayed on, and who were still here. He talked, smoked, and walked about the nine-foot-long space, while I sat on the edge of the bed and was curious as to what he actually did want to tell me, because it kept occurring to me that he was avoiding something—the very subject he was on the point of bringing up out there in the rain. All of a sudden he banged his fist on the partition at one end of the room, called "Bert!," then went to the other end where he called some other name, and when no answer sounded from anywhere, he sat down again, supported his head with his elbows on his knees and began to talk into space, not at me or even in my direction. No one really likes it here, they say, the days run on for everybody, yet one feels that he has a terrible amount of time, too much time. I knew about this. But I didn't expect it here, when I had actually been running away from it. What, Vilda went on, is one supposed to do with the time? Booze it up? Only that's worse, he'd tried that. But no, he doesn't intend to bore me. He begged me to forgive him, but it had occurred to him when I crossed his path for the second time, when I had seen him when old Kouba put him to shame, it had occurred to him I might tell him something, something other than what is customarily said here to someone in a bad mood: get a whore, have a drink, sleep as long as you like, bugger off.

Again he got up and walked about, shook his head, forced himself to smile and said: "So come here about half an hour before the flight briefing. We've got fine lads here, you'll see." He shook hands and showed me to the door. Vilda never told anybody the whole story. That evening we were to fly over Stuttgart. It was to be his twelfth mission. He didn't come to the briefing. Whenever, during the instructions of the information officer, the door of the dining room would open, our whole table would look in that direction. But I had enough to do to come to grips with that which was different here from my earlier service. Our pilot went in search of our commander, but returned after a half an hour and only shrugged his shoulders. At the end of the briefing a buzz arose in the dining room. At the tables in front of us the officers were whispering. One of them went up to the blackboard and wiped off Vilda's name from our crew; instead he wrote in the name of the wing commander. He turned to us and said we were to come to see him immediately after the briefing. He said nothing more that we could understand. He turned away our questions with the assertion that he himself knew nothing. Then there was no time for anything. I learned everything only after the mission was over. We climbed out, each one as if incognito, as if he did not want the others to see him, bent over the ground, and touched it with the flat palm of his hand. Mechanically we lit cigarettes, loosened our vests and the laces on our clumsy shoes. In the direction from which we had come it was beginning to dawn. More planes landed, in the air there was a booming noise, but we were already walking slowly toward the barracks. The commander stopped and gathered all six of us around him. He thanked us briefly and said that it had gone very well. He paused and then explained to us why he had flown with us. Captain Kotas had been found, half an hour before the briefing, dead, near the airfield.

It is dawn now. The birds are twittering, in the greasy fog the light of the next day is starting to penetrate, we can already hear the milkmen as their milk bottles clink against the thresholds of the homes, and it occurs to me, as I look at the pale face of my wife who is here beside me on the sofa sleeping, it occurs to me that Vilda escaped from it all in the only way that was, for him, in those circumstances, possible. He did not want to kill. You will say, obviously, that others had to do that for him. All right, I won't make an object lesson of him, a model or a religion. Such things are as hateful to my spirit as they were no doubt to him. In any case I completed my flying career. Now I sell raincoats, I have a family and, strangely enough, my occasional thoughts about Vilda Kotas neither frighten me nor do they undercut my zest for life.

Sincerely yours,

Pavel Sykora

A Speck of Truth

"Hi there! Do you have a minute? Just a speck of time—not even five minutes—a couple of seconds. Can you give me a couple of seconds? It's about that twenty-year anniversary celebration. Didn't you get your invitations yet? This has to be a big one. Just imagine what a reaction it got. All thirty-eight of you responded. Some others are dead, of course. We used to be forty-two. And you're to make the opening address."

A couple of seconds. Of course some died. There's static in the receiver, a light droning, an optimistic, talkative voice promising everything.

"You can't really refuse. You'll have it ready in a few moments." Fates. Brief, ardent, contorted, some near their end. Four of them. In a few seconds between picking up the receiver and putting it down. In a crackling and light droning.

Widened eyes, pale torpid fingers, half-opened lips. Surprise at the coming end. But nothing's begun yet. It was only a movement compelled by something from without. A bald, oval head from behind the lectern.

"Kafka, come here."

Slow footsteps between the benches, the smell of carbolic acid, the damp rag at the blackboard, and the chalk. Kafka looks around right and left.

"Give me a hint, fellows . . ." he whispered.

"Do you have your feet tied to your chair, Kafka?" the head asked from behind the lectern.

"No, excuse me, I haven't."

The forty-one others breathe their share of air, they have their own blood circulating, their own lowered eyes, they have their tedious morning emptiness. Only one head is huddled over so that it should not be visible from the teacher's desk, and is ready to prompt him. Kafka looks around and cocks his eye.

"Guys, don't let me get stuck with this."

The lectern asks: "Habeas Corpus Act."

The concealed head foxily protrudes forward. At the blackboard Kafka shifts his weight back and forth, a forlorn traveler at the last station in the world. Then he hears whispering. He can't see the mouth that whispers. He might be able to figure out what it's saying, but he can't see who is doing the whispering.

"The right—Kafka, do you hear—the right of the lords—"

"The right of the lords, the right of the lords," he repeats and turns his gaze toward the indifferent emptiness settled in the rows of heads from where the single thin voice is coming.

"To all—Kafka, say something—to all the maidens on the estate."

Kafka straightened up. Now he was dazzling. He spoke easily and with style.

"You were asking, Professor, what the Habeas Corpus was. Obviously it's the right of the lords to choose any girl on their estate they desire, for their own pleasure."

The head that prompted him shot out over the other heads. It laughed a loud, hiccuping laugh.

"Sit down," the lectern said.

Sit down, they told them when they brought them there. The wide-open eyes looked about. Don't leave me here, they said. The emptiness of the last hour under the low ceiling gave them the answer. Habeas Corpus, he said softly to himself. I know it, Professor. A whiff of gas puts him to sleep. Just like the morning lesson with the smell of carbolic, chalk, wet rags. I know it. One bowed head laughs hysterically. I know it, Professor, and Kafka gets up with his last strength. Don't laugh, you swine, I know it. And slowly he collapses, head downward, onto the cement floor. Someone's hand lifts his head, still alive, and delicately places it on his lap.

"Understand, at the beginning of that talk you should say what was waiting for us. That it wasn't an easy time. I'm not holding you up? Just a moment. It did make us break up, but now, when we are together again, we ought to help each other more and in the future, be of service to each other, do you understand? That's what you should say!"

Be of service, in a couple of seconds. The bell would ring in a minute.

"Honzík," said a voice bottled up by a wide, twirling moustache, and an index finger moved in the expectant silence of the classroom. The hundred-times repeated ritual is to be repeated. Enslavement of one of the forty-two has become a permanent part of the schedule. It doesn't upset anyone. Honzík's family name is Klír and he is delegated to bring the large moustache his franks, on the double, while they're still hot. All *that* was embodied in the slow movement of the index finger. Come here, I'll put the money in your palm, then you run down the corridor, down the stairs, trot two blocks to the deli, tell the man in the brown, stained apron two hot franks with mustard, two slices of bread, no crusts. At a gallop back, deliver the franks and the change, bow—and go wherever you like for a couple of minutes until the bell rings again. The long days of the year, the moustache, the street, the galloping, the red-brown apron, the return. But today the school Ganymede doesn't get up. His idea is: I'm curious. And he smiles, seated straight up on his bench, at the beckoning index finger: the smile of an investigator just before the outcome. What will happen now? The index finger droops, the moustache moves in disquiet, eyes on the sight: I am looking. Two, four, ten, twelve eyes. The discovery is completed. Klír's smile fades. He knows his future. The gallop through the streets—only that is left. Unless he goes and bows, each time and ever again, then eternal flight through the streets is all that remains for him. He sits straight up, no longer smiling. Whoever transgresses the boundary of everyday rituals knows his own fate.

The bell rings. He sits up straight at his table. It's them. He bends over to the drawers. Flyers, books, forged IDs. He carries them over to the stove. But what to do with the weapon? For a second he places its mouth on his temple. No. His thought is: I'm curious about their ritual to take a life, when it becomes burdensome. He smiles at the door behind which the bell is ringing. And they have eyes, taking aim, and I look, four, ten, twelve. A thought is endless curiosity. The smile disappears, the thought persists: Don't succomb. What will happen then?

He goes to the door, pulls it open, two shots: his before theirs. Then down the stairs, the gallop through the streets, it's night, everyone has the shades drawn and there's nowhere to go back to. Curiosity fades. He has learned the lesson. Whoever steps out of line comes to know his own fate. Driven past endurance, he will put an end to it, still curious. He doesn't want the handkerchief over his eyes, he stands erect, against him the eyes taking aim and I look, eight, ten, twelve. One of them has a moustache and it moves in disquiet. The idea is: I am—

"Feuer!"

"Many things can be prevented, though, isn't that true? You should say that. Let's promise to hang together. Somehow. I don't want to hold you up, you understand what I'm saying. When do you think you'll have your speech ready? Sit down right away and you'll have it. Tomorrow?"

He was standing opposite the director in the dark of his office, paunchy at seventeen, propped up with the heftiness and wisdom of the ages.

"Klinger, speak out, we've got no time for your Jewish quibblings," the director roared out of his narrow, wrinkled face. "Were you there?"

"Yes."

"Did you see them make the lights swing?"

"Yes."

"Did you swing along with the lights?"

"Yes."

"Did you see Professor Skopal come in?"

"Yes."

"And what happened then?"

"He nearly fell—he was staggering so."

"Do you understand you must be punished?"

"It's hard, but still."

"Whose idea was it—speak up. To humiliate authority that way. I'll kick them out—the whole class. You can all go shovel manure, you louts. If you don't tell me, I'll have the whole class arrested, do you hear me?"

Klinger, powerful on his short legs, began to swing forward, then back, as they had done then under those swinging lights. They were trying out the relativity of human attention. Anyone who couldn't swing like the others must have vertigo.

"Stand straight!"

And when I swing alone, Klinger thought to himself, I feel vertiginous. He stood motionless.

"So you won't tell?"

"No."

"We know anyway, coward."

"Hardly, Director."

"It was you."

"You're lying on purpose, Director."

"Get out."

Out. And then again he comes out after two weeks in solitary confinement. It is spring, is it daytime, is it night? Monday, Thursday, Sunday. He doesn't ask. He walks on. Still armed with the remnants of his body, the last flashes of the wisdom of the ages. Whoever rocks alone feels vertigo. Walk straight forward. He raises his head. That same protracted crack in the corridor wall above the doors of the cells—a thread along which I will make my exit from the darkness of the underworld, he had thought weeks ago when they led him back from the hearing and in torment he had smiled with his beaten, swollen face. He hadn't told them. He would never tell who it was that used his place as a hideout.

"We've got him already, we know," they roared at him.

"You're lying," he answered and took the blows.

"We'll let you go when you tell us."

"Not likely," he answered.

And when he went back along that thread on the wall, he told himself: It may be more than the wisdom of the ages. Dad would have bowed and said: Please, I'm not aware of that, excuse me. Uncle Ota would have said: Please allow me; I may be able to remember it. Aunt Klara—Aunt Klara can blubber Niagaras of tears in her own defense and she lurks under them and tells herself: Well then, has he given up? But she would hardly have won this.

Again the same corridor, but his smile had disappeared, his head was sinking. He staggered, and the walls swayed. I must be silent, I must be silent, he told himself. But his voice was too weak and he couldn't count on it. To be able to fill his lungs with fresh air, then lie down and sleep behind drawn shutters an endlessly long time, then get up, go to the store, again say: Mr. Krejčí, wipe off that dust on the shelves, please—cleanliness is our best salesman. But the store doesn't have to be. Mr. Krejčí can turn his back as he actually had. His apartment doesn't have to be. Only the air and the sidewalk and the café. Even the café doesn't have to be. Only the air and a bit of space around it. He doesn't hold it against Franz Kohn that he stayed, instead of going next door. The concièrge was a real dragon, and she couldn't sleep thinking he had another Jew up in his room. Nor did he hold anything against her. One day she too would sway and it would seem to her that the world was collapsing. To have air and open space, that would stop the vertigo. But it persisted. Even when the door opened in front of him and a narrow, wrinkled face rose up instantly.

"It's OK, Klinger."

It wasn't a smile, but now it wasn't a roaring beast either. The man walked around the desk and took Klinger by the arm.

"Come on, fellow, pick up your things and go home. We aren't so bad as we look sometimes. No. Anyone who's not guilty of anything gets along all right with us."

He led him out of the office and down the corridor, along the thread leading out of the underworld. They weren't going back to the cell, they were going someplace else, to the exit.

"The porter has your things; change your clothes there. What do you think of matters now, Klinger? Go home."

And he swayed, even though the arm supported his arm. The world is breaking up, the walls are moving apart. Aunt Klara will say: "Karlík!" and hide her dismay in floods of tears. Uncle Ota: "I told you they weren't as bad as people say." Dad will be ashamed of his show of emotion, turn partly away and say: "We haven't got the store anymore, you know that. What'll you do?" And he'll lie down and sleep and then go out freely, freely, onto the sidewalk. They had passed through the gratings, improbability was beginning to take on the color of reality, and he swayed with vertigo.

"Why, Klinger, what's wrong with you, take hold of yourself, go home. It's just time for a bite. I'll lend you some money; around the corner there's a place to eat. Just so you don't go home famished, they're not expecting you. We aren't so bad, are we?"

The wisdom of the ages is weak. This doesn't belong to the sort of things it has experienced. Klinger trembled and swayed.

"You haven't done anything bad. Or that night visitor of yours. You can be calm and tell us what his name was, and you can go home."

Dad, Uncle Ota, and the soft, lined weeping Aunt Klara.

"Who?" his living vertigo asks.

"That friend of yours. It was fun for you to talk all night long with him about the good old times, right? About girls, about boozing."

"What do you mean—Franz Kohn and girls!"

The sound of that name stopped his vertigo. With clenched fingers Klinger covered his face and the kick propelled him back to the grating and inside it. They were taking him down the straight, cruelly straight, corridor to his cell. Behind him there was laughter. Klinger had no time, no strength to raise his eyes to the crack, to the thread high up on the corridor wall. The wisdom of the ages knew there was no necessity for that. Why remember the way out of the underworld when one never comes back from there, even if he should survive?

"So they can rely on you, right? Will you do it? I knew I wouldn't be disappointed in you. It'll be wonderful when we do get together. Just think, everyone will make it—except for them of course. Oh well. I didn't hold you up very much, did I? Goodbye then."

The bell had stopped ringing. But thoughts race on. It's hard and who would know it. *Epistulae ex Ponto*, their sense and meaning. Only Horák, the one with a moustache under his nose and freckles all over, finished writing. Concisely, grandly, with perfect command. Let no one bawl at home with Mama or *ex Ponto*, all the same he'll die. Horák's a troublemaker, they say. He drinks, has a moustache, he's a skirt-chaser, and he gets topnotch grades. He's the first to close his exam book. Karásek, with spectacles, flabby, sits next to him.

"Wait," he hisses. "I haven't got it yet."

"Get it, you monkey, I'd like a cigar."

In the front of the classroom the scourge of mankind dozes. When he doesn't nap, he does earn his title.

"Write; I'm going to dictate," Horák whispers and crumples a cigarette between his fingers: "His appeal to his friends appears to have been in vain, for in the year seventeen—write it down, monkey, it's taking you ages—in the year seventeen A.D. Ovid died and prophesied his own death, since the last verse—Karásek, you're a suicide, can anyone write that way? make an effort, you ape—the last line sounds—have you got it?—*omnia perdidimus*—"

The scourge of mankind awoke and sailed into the aisle.

"Has the bell rung yet, you scum?" he roared.

Hesitation.

"Don't tell lies, you riff-raff! Turn in your papers!"

"How did you say that?" Karásek begged, concealed behind the shoulders of the one sitting in front of him, sunken, hidden. He would have liked to sit still lower. Not to exist. God, what was in store for him now? Slaps, his glasses on the floor, his monster father would kick him again, and his Mama: "Are you surprised? Just let him have it, the idiot; he gets it from you, the beast." While his mama and father start to bicker, he picks up the broken china, skulks away nearer to the end of his life. God, if it were only here. With a smarting of the eyes but without tears. Where would he find them, anyway, after so much? Used to the strap, the dog of the family, the dog of the school class, the Karásek of mankind. "Wait—*omnia*—how was it?"

"*Perdidimus*, Karásek, understand. *Per-di-di-mus*," the scourge guffawed over him.

"Collection time, do you hear?" the trusty appears among the bunks. "The mail collection won't wait. A month from now you can finish up your novels— now we're collecting."

Karásek stretched his neck. The giraffe, they called him. He had lost his glasses forever, and he was reinforcing his vision bysticking out his long skinny neck from his striped blouse that was too big for him just as there was too much of the world for him. How did you come to be here? they asked him at the very first. He replied by shrugging his shoulders. And one of them said to him: "Aren't you van der Lubbe?" In bed at night he remembered who that was. He'd heard the name somewhere. A notorious judicial error, Roubal had said about him, without mocking him, with kindness, the only one who was kindly, not really with them, withdrawn from them at times of jokes, complaints, of imaginary cooking, close in times of illness. Karásek was sitting behind him and extending his neck over the lines and script of his letter. He felt anxious and empty. Not to exist, to escape his own stench, to submerge himself, to rest forever away from the dogskin with which he was flogged at home, flogged from the abrupt changes here. One single, thin dream is in him: thinly, silently to slit open his veins. And the blood would have run, he told himself, when everyone walked past him and he was not even a dog—just air and emptiness. Only Roubal. And he copied from his page.

"Dearest Mom and Dad, the thought of your tenderness and closeness is very encouraging to me. Please, I don't want you to pity me. I'll come out of it stronger, believe me, and if I don't come out, even then it will have been worth it. I've known you for twenty-three years, people who are worthy of being called human beings. I want to be worthy of you, and forgive me my pride when I write that it's here that I have the greatest chance to be worthy of you and sometimes I think that I will succeed in availing myself of that chance. If you can, send me warm socks in your next package, and a sweater. Winter's coming. I'll do everything to get through it, for your sakes, for my friends, for the fact that I want to live. If a letter doesn't come next time, remember that you don't need to be ashamed of me, and don't grieve either. Unless we lose ourselves, we have lost nothing, not even through death. Kisses."

Word for word, with the same forms of the letters, Karásek fills out the void of the lines. With his thin dream of a thin cutting silenced for the time. He rubs his eyes, his dry, reddened eyes, which read with such effort in the dim light. In the middle of a word he stops, again he rubs his eyes. They are, for the first time in a century, damp. He throws his arms on Roubal's shoulders.

"Roubal, I'm lying," he weeps on his neck.

The trusty has picked up his sheet of paper.

"We have lost nothing," he reads and guffaws. "Without your glasses, eh, Karásek? Don't mind, in a year they'll come for you, real Zeiss glass from Jena. And outside life. That'll come too, giraffe, you'll live to see it."

"Give that here," Roubal suddenly stands in front of the trusty.

Heads turned from their bunks.

"Look, the defender of widows and orphans," the trusty laughs, and waves Karásek's letter in front of Roubal's nose. Roubal grabs his hand.

"Don't be a fool, Roubal," men call out all around and some of them jump forward. They grab Roubal from behind and the trusty has the time to break his nose.

Karásek whips around, jumps onto the trusty's neck with the thin thought: I'll be your equal. He hits, kicks, bites the trusty. And then he flies, thrown halfway down the aisle between the rows of bunks, and the top of his head hits a column. The impact and the final thin thought: Roubal, let's have just—a tiny speck of truth.

The Sources
of History

"*When from all of us there will be only shadows.*"
—Jaroslav Seifert

September 21, 1937

Markétka, things are going better and better with me, I'm teaching in the village school in Hladková and soon will take my exam to teach in municipal school. Why did our poor mother have to die, she would have been so proud of me. I've made friends with the school inspector, Mr. Pivoda, and he's looking out for me. I want to invite him to come home for a slaughtering—please get ready for our visit. We're living through such stirring times, though they may be unhappy. Our people will not perish when they can unite so grandly as we see them do. When the coffin with our beloved president's body came past, we all knelt on the spot. Yes, Markétka, you too would have had tears in your eyes and you would have said, "We shall ever be faithful." So you and Véna get ready for me to come next time, not by myself as usual, but with the school inspector. And fatten up the hog. Your Jan.

July 5, 1938

Markétka, the glorious days are upon us, and I keep thinking of you and how you're all getting ready for the harvest. I'd have invited you for the great days of our national festival, so you could have a look and see how grandly Prague can entertain its providers from the countryside, but we aren't as well off as we would like, and you know how a new household is always in need of something. At least I can send you a picture of the Sokol Parade. If you could only have heard the shouting. Otylka says it was thunderous, and just let anyone try and interfere with our liberties. She is such a patriot; I couldn't have found a better wife. I'll come and see you sometime and bring her with me, so you can get to know her. When do you have the slaughtering, anyway? I've forgotten. All the best, and glory to the Great Sokol Congress. Your Jan.

March 16, 1939

Markétka, a thousand thanks for the sausage. I don't know what we would have done without you. It's sleeting all the time, and you in the country certainly know that we have been occupied. But Otylka and I keep saying that we don't need to hang our heads in shame, the way some people do: for instance, my fellow teacher Dosoudil, who jumped out of the window when he saw that mighty and well-disciplined German Army march in. Otylka says that we have only one life to live, and I agree with her. We'll see what comes next, but I think that a small people can only benefit from the help a great people can bestow. Give my best to Véna and keep him on a leash—he's such a wild man. Tell him for me to keep his mind on the farm, it will pay better than other things he could try—but you understand, I can't write about it. Otylka sends her greetings and is looking forward to another package. She remembers you both with pleasure. For both of us, your Jan.

July 30, 1942

Markétka, a few firebrands have put our nation in terrible danger of being wiped out, and I am all the more unhappy in that I can't make my pupils understand, because their irresponsible parents raise their children to remember those elements who thought so unrealistically that a small people like us can afford to have its own so-called ideals. Before I can even get to the heart of the matter they begin stamping. Only two or three of them do it, but the others are cowards and cover it up. We have a hard life now, but I do have faith that under the heavy blows of fate people will come to understand where our place is. I'm sorry for what you write about your husband, but I hope that now you too will understand what course our thinking must take. Otylka supposes your husband must have deserved it in part, and I have to agree with her, because I do know him. Let's hope that in his case justice will blink its eyes. Even though it will be a great loss for us, I understand that now for a while you won't be able to send us anything. Keep a stiff upper lip. Your Jan.

May 20, 1945

Markétka, a new day is dawning on the wreck of the past, and as though dazzled by the glow of a new freedom we still don't know what to do next. But when Otylka and I welcomed, amid the roaring crowds, our new president—how gray he's gotten over all those years, poor fellow—we thought of you, and how wonderful you feel now that Véna's come back. I know his hastiness very well—he's such a strange fellow—and I won't even take it to heart that he got the idea of spoiling Otylka's and my joy in these historic days with that letter that he sent us. You probably didn't read it, because I refuse to believe that you could have been on his side in this. You know very well that all of us have suffered without distinction, each in his own way, except that a few only were given to win honor and happiness by having the opportunity to show their courage in deeds. Véna used very strong expressions, and at first Otylka and I supposed we would never be able to forgive him, but we finally decided we could forget it since he is an ordinary man. His rough character has never had a chance to be polished or to be brought into the regulated flow of civilized humanity, as we have. Tell him that he should remember the words of our President Masaryk, that a democracy has to reckon with people who are wrong. And who of us isn't wrong? We hope the trains soon start running so we can look in on you again. Otylka sends her greetings. Your Jan.

March 1, 1948

Dear Markétka, life in Prague is returning again to its normal ways after the February events. We members of the working intelligentsia can only rejoice that the takeover planned by those rightist scoundrels, who tried to pass themselves off as a democratic idealists, came to failure. Otylka is calling to me from the kitchen to ask whether you don't happen to have a few onions left over from winter. She hates standing in line so. You know, we're not so young any more, and can't stand in line the way young people do. I wish you could have lived through the excitement when the two of us stood for whole hours in the dense crowds on Wenceslaus Square, that place that has already seen so many stirring historical times, and waited for Chairman

Gottwald to return from the Castle and announce the president's decision. We are now in wise hands, and if we stand honestly alongside the working class, so impressive in its strength, nothing can happen to us. Otylka has already applied for Party membership, and we may even have luck and push my membership through somehow. You know, the needs of my job made me join another party, but you yourself can witness that I've always been on the side of the people. As for Véna, he'll certainly be glad the way things have gone. He always was such a radical. Give him greetings from both of us. Your Jan and Otylka.

July 3, 1948

Markétka, you're such a good-hearted soul, it really pains me to have to return this parcel to you, the one you sent us by your husband. It will all be spoiled in this hot weather. I have to write to you without Otylka knowing, because she's terribly angry at both of you and might not even let me. She has such strong principles, and your husband really offended her. No, you shouldn't have sent him to see us, when you know what his character is like. And so it's really your fault. Understand me, Markétka, I too was touched by that mighty Sokol parade that so loudly proclaimed loyalty to those old ideas in which we were all raised. I too had tears in my eyes, but they were tears of pity for so many peo-

ple seduced. I myself have already fought through
my inner battle, while those deluded crowds still
have theirs to fight. And now you send your husband to see us. He grinned at our Party badges as
soon as he was in the doorway and even dared say
that one day we'd take them off again. I couldn't
stop Otylka from telling him that he should go
preach on the street and not in our house. It's true
he didn't really preach, but you can certainly understand Otylka's exasperation when you realize
what a person of principles she is. I couldn't have
found a better wife, and so with pain in my heart
I'm returning all these things and informing you
that in the future we must break off all relations
with you. Otylka says that you might threaten our
position, and I must agree with her. Jan Stavinoha.

June 20, 1955

Dear Markétka, we were criticized in our local
Party organization for not being ready to take anyone
in for the Spartacade, so we told them that you were
coming to stay with us. Otylka says she doesn't want
anybody else to stay here, because they could be
disorderly and we would have to keep our eye on
them every minute. You know what those athletes
and their friends are like. You know how different
people can be, even if they aren't bad Communists.
So we're inviting the two of you, Véna too, most sincerely, and if you should bring anything with you

when you come we would be most happy, because the stores here are full of shoppers and it's simpler that way. Please do come and let us count on you, because we have a Party worker here in the building and she could tell them if we didn't take anybody in. She knows more about us than we do ourselves. The two of you shouldn't think that my personal views are the same as those in the newspapers. There are a lot of things that are quite different from the way they appear. I look forward to talking all that over with Véna. He's such a sensible person, and I often think of him. Otylka may be a bit tight-lipped—she didn't get to go to the regional meeting of the Defenders of Peace as they originally promised, so she's bitter. But I'm looking forward to your coming and the heartfelt talk we'll have; I can't tell you in a letter. So definitely, please do come as soon as possible. We don't have to go to the Spartacade if we don't want to, just so we'll fulfill our obligation and they won't give us trouble needlessly in the Party. We look forward to seeing you and send you all our love. Your Jan and Otylka.

The Letter

At first it looked as if they would go to that party at the Autoclub after all; but when they had come down Chotek Highway and didn't take the road across Letná Plain and over Holešov Bridge to Vysočany and from Vysočany straight home to Horní Počernice, when instead of that they had crossed Mánes Bridge, all of a sudden the boss had turned off along the embankment to František Square, to Denisák and taken the underpass to Královská Avenue—the last two named after men of those fabulous times when only Masaryk was Masaryk, and instead of Socialist Youth we had Boy Scouts or, at worst, Sokols. What could Tom do? He had to stay with the boss. Or would he be permitted to go to the Autoclub himself?

Last spring was different. Then there was a party at the Autoclub, and it looked as if the boss might rise into the circles of the people who matter. Quite calmly he entertained himself with Lučák, with Bishop, with Rosák, with Killmayer and the others. When he didn't get on well with somebody, they would somehow bump backs with each other. That was the way it looked, even though the boss had only come in third in the last race. But this year?

Tom thought: To hell with this bumpy road. He clenched his teeth and stepped on the gas, because the boss, on his old Indian, had opened up and there was fear of losing the sidecar; in other words, one extra wheel, some tubing, and a beaten-down floor with a place for anchoring his racing cycle.

Just as they reached Palmovka, the boss again confused Tom. He turned left and downhill across the railway gates to Libeň. At Sokolovna he braked, turned off into the alley leading to Rokytka, and stopped. With the fingers of his left hand Tom unbuckled, in a sign of rage, sorrow, protest, he didn't quite know what, with his right, clasped palm on the rotating handle he revved his squeaking, rebuilt 1935 vintage Sarolea three or four times, accelerating to madcap, daredevil velocities. Then he too stopped his machine.

"Leave that here and let's go," said the boss. He was dressed the same as when he had been racing up above at Strahov: in high boots, all in leather, a cap instead of a helmet. Around his neck a multicolored scarf with a bright red border stuck out a bit sloppily. "Just pick up your suitcase and let's go."

Tom propped the Sarolea on its footrest against the sidewalk and looked to see where they might possibly be going. My God! "Kaplan's Pub" was written there in faded green handwriting on the gray wall. A two-storied, decrepit building with a low, brown door. In the upper part behind glass panes hung dirty lace curtains. The lace was torn in places.

The boss stepped forward, and in the middle of a second step braked with his metal-sheathed left sole. For a moment it appeared as if he was not going to drag Tom into this evident fall from glory, after all.

"They can go to hell! Even the cottage where I was born is communal today. Here, when I was an apprentice, I got drunk for the first time—so much so that it was almost for the last time, too."

Tom halted his work of unloading the suitcase from the cycle, in case he was going to have to fasten it right back on again.

"Old Kaplan probably won't be at home now." He even made an attempt to influence his boss.

"What do you know about any Kaplans? Hurry up. Pečenka has lived here as a subtenant for at least twenty years now. Old Lojza. You have to distinguish, because young Lojza—you wouldn't even want to know about it. They say he pays alimony for five families, average two kids apiece. Some even say for seven. The poor old man, old Lojza, was soft on him and took care of the grandchildren the best he knew how, but how could he be up to it, when Lojza—understand, the young one—didn't have time to work. But if you tried to hint at this, you were booted out of the house. That crap on the windows is from his time. Let's go."

In the low front room there stood behind the bar a

dry, tall man, a bit hunched in the back of his neck, his face full of thin, deep wrinkles, adorned on top with the lock of hair pushed from the crown down onto his forehead. Behind him, an immeasurably stout woman, clad in a sweatsuit, was rummaging in the drawer of an antique sideboard. The man responded to their greeting, but even then his motionless eyes clung to the foam sputtering from the tap.

"I'm going down for another keg, take the bar for me," he turned his head (but on no account his eyes) to the woman. "If the gentlemen want light beer, let them sit and wait," he added impersonally, bent down toward the narrow door beside the sideboard, and you could hear how circumspectly, step after step, he descended to the cellar.

The woman did not turn away from her work in the drawer. "Would you gentlemen care for anything?" she asked.

Tom stood to the side and saw how a prettily twisted curl of hair drooped now and then onto the knives and forks she was tidying in the drawer. A sweatsuit—the hag! To be as fat as that in it. But then she wasn't really ugly. Even now she wasn't. Only in the rear. Jenka would never let herself go like that.

The boss was looking elsewhere, at the four seated men in the corner. They had a small table pushed up against their table. The small table held their beers, while they played cards in scowling silence. The man at the head, his face toward the entrance, slowly lifted his damp, pallid gaze, slapped his last card on the pile, and then pulled the whole pile in for himself. All four sighed at once, three of them reached out for their beers, and the fourth began to shuffle the cards. Habit permitted him to look up, while shuffling with a kind of half-closed facial expression, at a yellowish light bulb hanging below a milky shade in the middle of the low ceiling. Here there was nothing but twilight. Gottwald and Stalin looked down from the gray wall, just as expressionless and burned-out as the players in the corner. Let's hope forever, it struck Tom.

The green language of the poster alongside the entrance door announced that the Cinema Sofia was playing *The Unforgettable Year*. And which year was that? Another, now quite shabby poster higher up near the ceiling proclaimed: with the Soviet Union. Really? What and whose eternity did they have in mind? If the Socialist Youths' future is meant, in two or three years it would turn pale like their shirts. You go on to better shirts, or you don't. Or are they thinking of the Czechoslovak Church Forever of Pastor Kralíček? That is, tiny like he is, and odd like his family name. Over the door leading to the next room, cold darkness peered out of its glass panes, and a strip of paper, once perhaps white, was nailed up. They must have nailed it up there overzealously, too soon after painting. The drying, grayish, old rose paint, of the lowest quality, had pressed through the paper so as to destroy almost totally the legibility of the text, itself possibly originally red. But Tom didn't feel like hunting for authority underneath the word. Or rather, underneath the blabbering. He knew from elsewhere that there, stubbornly, impersonally, illegitimately and audaciously, it was now known for whom. The authorities had had its text printed: I vote for peace. There was no mention of who should handle the negotiations.

The boss hung his cap up on the coat hook on the wall and sat down on a bench in a corner as far from the cardplayers as possible. Tom pushed away his chair with its plywood back, on which the wood's pressed designs gleamed dully, and slowly began to push the table, which rocked either because of one short leg or because the plank floor wasn't level. And for this you work for weeks and far into the night on your machine the best you can—and then risk breaking your neck. To be on the noisy carousel of fleeting glory. And sometimes instant oblivion.

The table in the corner wasn't far from the tavernkeeper's rear, since the room was in fact exactly equal in size to a small house. The boss didn't even have to shout when he ordered.

"Any goulash, Miss?"

"No—nothing. Only salami off ration, twenty crowns for ten dekas, if you've got it." She spoke with a hint of an older, silken affability, reinforced with schooling.

With Jenka nothing must be old, Tom thought as he looked about, listened, and reflected. Life mustn't

touch her—or what would it do to her? Cover her
with a crust. Soil her. He must teach her!

"Let's have it: two plates," the boss said politely,
but with force. "And what can we drink? We don't
want beer."

The woman, who had already spent too much time
over the drawer, perhaps from a distaste for looking
life squarely in the face, began to reel off the list.

"We've got first-class Curaçao, chocolate liqueur,
rum, if you please, cognac—no, we've run out, I
think—Karlík's coming right back, he can tell you
everything. Are you in a big hurry, gentlemen?"

The boss wasn't listening anymore. He rubbed his
face with both palms, absentmindedly he drew a
piece of broken comb from the pocket of his leather
vest and ran it through his thick, dark hair. There
was little about him that girls and ladies around thirty could turn down without suffering a twinge.

But still, Tom thought, maybe this evening would
turn out well. True, he would rather have been
dancing with Jenka at The Růžek, to the three-man
band. In vain he attempted to clean his nails with
the tip of his pocket knife. The oily stuff stuck on, as
if he had not even touched it. We should have
placed higher in the race. Compared to the others,
they had come out of the curves like a snail. But the
boss had said no. Tom should leave it as it is. And
then the Jap: the real Jap OHC with its chrome cas-
ing for the chain for driving the camshaft. When he
starts going on about that, Jenka's eyes turn toward

the ceiling. Such a sharp guy and even he can be caught by such toys. But you can ride those toys, Jenka darling—I know, you saw there in your first year of practical training the idiotic consequences of those Japs and everything like that. But it's really the result of using them in an idiotic way! With a Jap like that, a genuine Jap—it had to have cost a pretty penny! It wouldn't hurt to have a good wash all over, Tom told himself and scratched under his shirt where he felt an itch from the dried-up sweat accumulated throughout the day. When that machine is warmed up a bit and goes off, it won't catch again. Either it's a hundred percent or nothing. Jenka, I know what's wrong with it. I had told the boss before our last ride out we'd better leave it running. Better to overheat it than let it cool off halfway. Then they were hurrying to get there before dark. But the boss had said no. Turn it off. And then Tom couldn't catch his breath when he was pushing round and round in a circle in the station, and nothing, not even a sound. Not even the boss was good for anything, anymore. Fed up with the world, probably for his own particular personal reason. Most likely Božka. She was opposed to the rules of the game in the station. She must have given someone a hundred or more. When was that? Right after the first ride. That was when he'd first seen them together. The boss hadn't picked any flaming beauty. Now he looked at the boss out of the corner of his eye. A fellow like the boss could have a dame like

Jenka—but not Jenka, because that wouldn't be his style. And he liked Božka—

The boss awoke from his fixed gaze at the card-players. "Well, lady, will you give us something or did we wander by mistake into the station waiting room?"

"It's coming right up—you're in a big hurry, gentlemen?" She turned her head from the drawer but still lingered over it.

"Reach into the sideboard and pour us two slivovitzes. Use brandy glasses. You do have slivovitz in there?"

A noise of trampling sounded from the cellar, and the tall man with the long forelock bent his head and entered the room.

"Why don't you serve them anything, good Christ!" he roared and walked straight to the tap on the right. He turned the handle and it began to sputter anew, this time more vigorously, with a hint of promise.

"They want slivovitz, Dad, have we got slivovitz?" The woman slid the door closed and spoke over her shoulder. It was possible that she had once been a beauty and so now all the worse for the tavern-keeper. Her eyes in her fleshy face seemed to be too close to each other, and her nose somehow too high up.

"Well, take a look, for God's sake," the tavern-keeper said without looking at her. "There's too much of you. More beer, gentlemen?" He raised his head toward the cardplayers, and from imperceptible signs he comprehended the answer since he knew the routine, so with intense concentration he drew the beers some fractions of a second early. The woman was almost entirely sunken behind the bar, as she bent over toward the lower doors of the cupboard, and of her there could be seen only her oval back. It struck Tom that they were lion-tamers with a whip and a magnificent creeping lioness: not in the ring anymore, but at home in a circus wagon a half century after the final applause. Jenka better never get the idea of getting that fat. Uneasy, he arose and walked to the bar. Meanwhile the lioness straightened up, the extinguished remnants of age-old smiles were seen under the down of her moustache, and while staging a bravura performance in pouring she raised her eyes to Tom.

"Just sit, lad. There're two of you—I like to serve deuces. Do they still make money at the merry-go-round? I was afraid they'd close them down now—just like they did the churches—"

"I can't say for the priests, but the boss has enough to pay for this stuff," Tom pointed at the glasses and did whatever he could to smile or even try to laugh, only he was pained at how beauty can disappear. The future is darkness, it struck him—and then another thought: but what if another Jenka is born from Jenka!

But for whom, he thought when he brought the glasses back and set them down on the table. Someone like the boss wouldn't be nearly so mean. There are much worse—even if, well, who knows?

"You know what drinking's about, Tom?" the boss clinked with Tom's glass, which stood there straight and stiff, like Tom.

"I don't care much for this," Tom pulled up the chair beneath him.

"And what do you care for?"

The boss didn't wait for his answer. He drank down his glass at one gulp. Care, care, Tom thought, what would I care for—of course, besides Jenka and a couple of books, what she gets from her old widow mother and I get from my father out of his bookcase, so that then we argue whether *When It Rained All the Time* is nonsense, or the *Fairy Tale of May* is unreadable after two pages, and Jindřich Jindřich Baar—how they crammed us full of him in school the way they did with Jirásek, an old graybeard who bores you to death after fifteen minutes—I'd rather have a Jap machine like the boss's, he'd look at me differently then.

"Bartovský dropped by the day before yesterday." The boss twisted his empty glass in his fingers, then gave that up and nervously stuck his half-empty pack of Lípas under Tom's nose. "Here, smoke one. We've got to start fixing his antique Lejda. Right away tomorrow."

I'd like to see that, Tom thought. He wanders off by nine already—God knows where—all those jammed nozzles get left on my back, each oiled clutch that rides along the Poděbrady highway, all the safety belts that ever get torn there. There's no time left to do a decent job. That was something, last year before spring, when Vojtěchovský brought in on the truck a broken-down Bugatti. Good Lord, I'd like to have a breakdown like that some time! No corrosion in the engine, not one burned-out valve, ballbearings as if they were still new. I'm sorry, Jenka—I almost forgot you. No, it won't happen again. They gave Vojtěchovský a job in Kopřivnice when he showed what he could do with the Bugatti. We won't even have Bartovský's Lejda to work on. But out loud Tom said little.

"We should."

He sat down and straightened his posture in the crook of his back. The inconspicuously vigilant lion-tamer silently came up to fill the boss's glass. He accepted as if he were far away in his thoughts, without a word, without a gesture. One of the cardplayers pushed his chair back with a rattling noise. The lioness sat down heavily on the chair behind the bar, placed her chin in her palm and glanced at the newspaper.

"Look," she said without looking up, "here's an ivory dinner service for sale, a leopard skin, a Liebermann, and a Leica—what's a Leica—shouldn't the word before be a Dobermann?" And her gaze moved on the page in an entirely different direction.

"Read only about things you can afford and things you can understand," said the tamer, without bothering to look at her, meanwhile engagingly transformed into a benign tavern-keeper, when with a relatively

clean rag he carefully cleaned the yellowed sheet
metal on the top of the bar. He rinsed out, in the tub
that was installed there, three half-liter glasses with
their remnants of foam, placed them bottoms up,
with folded arms leaned against the edge of the cupboard and, only half present, glanced at the cardplayers. Everything was as if it had happened here
long ago.

The glass in front of the boss was empty before
Tom had a chance to look. The way he drinks. . . it
occurred to him. He hadn't known that. Or perhaps
he had never wished to know it. Not even now. And
as if he felt guilty he bent his gaze above the left
outer pocket of his canvas lumber-jacket, which he
had put on over his sweater and his jeans and which
yesterday Jenka had had to repair at the seams so he
wouldn't be the shame of the Strahov stadium, and
he caught sight of a stiff light-brown rectangle of
paper on a rolled-up blue-and-white string. He read
what was printed on it. LONG FLAT-TRACK RACE, it
said. Below the date and below that, in red, ME-
CHANIC. Cautiously he untied the string so as not to
tear off the button—because for him the button was
Jenka—and thought: So it's just us, Jenka, this year
we're through with the races.

"Well, we're through with the races, Tom," the
boss said, placed his clenched fists on the table in
front of himself, one on top of the other, and
propped his chin on the pile. He too, hardly present,
gazed at the cardplayers, but continued to speak.

"Višňák from Hradec will have it, since he's so crazy to get it. Do you remember Čermná, how he went after her that time? If he'd had a hundred thousand, he'd have paid it then.

"For a Jap?" Slowly and unwillingly, Tom was coming back from far off.

The door with its tattered curtains squeaked, clicked shut, and behind Tom's back there sounded a child's voice.

"Good evening, Mr. Kunst, Dad wants the usual. I've got the money today."

They could hear the dying clatter of a clay jug and the pouring of coins on the bar. From the magically half-open tap in Libeň near Rokytka it began to sputter. Tom saw this only out of the corners of his eyes, but somehow the gesture impressed him. Or did it frighten him? He wasn't quite sure, so many repressed sufferings, and then so many fellows in a drunken stupor, with every hundred such gestures. Perhaps his father the upholsterer would have said it that way. It had never occurred even to him, pre-sumably, to wear a cap of the sort Masaryk wore. There was a time, even, when that cap almost looked something like Lenin's. In some ways his father thought the way Masaryk did, naturally. He did not need to show it outwardly.

"For heaven's sake, lads!" The superannuated li-oness got up, took the salami from under a glass bell on the sideboard, and began to slice it. "I'm sorry, I apologize, I'm here again doing this just for you."

"If he wants it, then he should have it," the boss spoke, now more and more focused, and decisive. And in case Mr. Kunst, once he got rid of the boy, should come with the bottle of slivovitz to pour, the boss extricated from the breast of his leather vest three crumpled hundred-crown notes, put them in his palm, and requested that the bottle remain on the table. "It has to leave home," he added then, when lion-tamer Kunst had withdrawn.

The Jap's alive, that's clear, it struck Tom. Only he talks about it as if it were a member of his family. And meanwhile the boss again smoothed down his hair, this time with only his stiffened, blackened fingers, and spoke straight out to Tom.

"Tomorrow we take it from him, and that's that."

"And how about Bartovský's Leyda?" Tom objected timidly.

"We've trained her to wait—just as the *lady* here has trained us," he said with a labored smile aimed up at the sweatsuited lioness. In a flash he thanked her, but pushed away the plate immediately, and only when she was far enough in the distance did he add in a muffled voice: "Do you know anything at all?—you know nothing about life, Tom."

Better be on the highway, Tom thought behind lowered eyelids. With Jenka behind. Or still up there. When they shift their weight forward a bit and move the machine a trifle so it starts to lean. Rosák, Mr. Engineer, lifts himself up the whole way as if he were trying to sit over the front wheel, like a circus performer, forward over the handlebars. Jenka has been saying for months now that she likes to go riding with me, not just watching. So in the end, already now, while I am young, I have to be a lion-tamer. Can no harmony last then, even during the daytime? The Young Communists are after her to come and dance with them. Naturally, at the Railway Station bar. Small talk about nothing. Jenka would rather go to sleep. In those awful blue Party shirts, poor guys. They gab about Wolker, Mayakovsky—but will they tell her and tell them all that the latter gave up, like my Dad the upholsterer told me, falling gracelessly to earth. Bang, bang, the way they taught us. Jenka, things are tough: In twenty minutes the boss'll most likely fall under the table, just as he supposedly does every other day at the Čelakovský Inn, on the right side just as you get on Poděbrady highway.

The cardplayers had just finished a round, and one of them, a tired, double-chinned man, the owner of a gourmet store or possibly of a less smelly but also less profitable haberdashery, went to that dark room in back and through it to some place more remote, from which mold and ammonia could be smelled. One could hear the noise of sputtering. Unhappily Tom couldn't tear his mind away, because he kept imagining at the very same time how the boss would sell it and, except for Jenka, everything would be over. Week after week, the whole year long, only to clean carburetors and distributors, change spark plugs and for a crown "tip" to buy beer, bow, and say thank you.

Idiots. Even if they give a hundred times as much, do they know what fun it is to adjust the valves and the ignition so that it races and pulls in regular intervals the best it can? You can't pay for that sort of thing. Just like you can't pay for a Jap.

"Boss, keep the Jap," said Tom.

"That's silly, Tom, you don't know anything," the boss answered so loud that the cardplayers slowly raised their faces. But at once they turned back to their cards. The former lioness was half dozing over the newspapers. The lion-tamer, from under his remaining head of hair, with a feigned lack of interest, followed his last two customers and was evidently adding up in his head what the day would bring.

"Look here, Tom: these hands," the boss went on more quietly.

"I was only thinking that if I could I would," said Tom and only then did he look at the boss's hands. They were not the hands of an idle man.

"If only you could earn enough money to buy it? With those corroded distributors and the film on the battery contacts? And the clientele all skinflints? Don't fantasize."

With time, that's clear, only with time, why not? Tom thought. And they didn't slap me either, not even when my upholsterer father said, at least twice, aloud: Do you need a slapping? It wouldn't even occur to me. I need my hand for finer work, but if you do try anything, then I can give it to you under the chin, right where it counts. Just remember,

you're our only child because Mama gave up fifty
years before she had to—let Mama forgive, no, she
didn't give up, she simply passed away, because at
that time there were no medicines for what she had.
And I'm no worse than they were, either in my
hands or my head. If I was, would the boss have
chosen me from the crowd of applicants to be his
right arm? But if he does sell it, for a whole year
there'll be an oil pit and a view of the rust of the
wrecks underneath, and no prospect of a race taking
me off somewhere or even a horse that would ride
under me. Only nozzles, Young Communists, and
ragtag soccer behind the Old Sokol Hall will be left.

"See these hands?" The boss looked to make sure
that he returned to the present, but his voice was
again resonant and he employed more expressive
movements of the hands, to which he had called attention. "See them? They didn't earn shit!"

The boss bent back, and with a kind of laborious
calm poured out the last drink for Tom and himself.
The diminution within the bottle was quite percepti-
ble, and the boss's eyes were, in spite of the effort
mentioned, a bit unfocused. Balloons in a light
breeze. But all the same Tom was somewhere near
the center of his blotted vision.

"Tom, if you've got the scratch, it's yours. It
works, it only needs a fresher driver in the saddle.
Keep it. A Jap has to get out—because of her I want
to—because of her I have to—damn it, Tom, pre-
tend you don't know anything!"

He took Tom's left fist in his rather strong right hand and turned it around, as if he would let it go completely after two-thirds of a revolution.

"Did you notice how Božka came there today—anyway, you know what happened."

Tom gazed at the green-and-white checkered tablecloth, wonderfully clean for a fifth-category tavern converted from a hut, but suddenly he felt nauseated. Just like one of the boys spreading his bread thick with oil during training. He bit into it, and once was enough. It was a rancid brown oil collected in an oblong pan from the crankcase of some old wreck. Every morning at half-past five on his way to lectures or practicum he'd always stop when he went by Aunt Nalka's; she lived in the house next door, and she'd give him something between morning snack and lunch. This time it was a sandwich: three luscious pieces of last evening's roast goose between fresh slices of bread. With the added oil they left only the bones from the meat. Jenka was fourteen then and wore her braids clasped together in the embarrassing form of ladybugs. Only, just as she will never be swollen up or withered like fifty-five-year old Mrs. Kunstová, nor was she ever a giggling, unruly fourteen, and the silly ladybugs forced on her by her widowed mother she had magisterially overcome. Just like the way I must have been a first-class bore when I came back home that evening to the village, because I still felt like shit, but she'd wait for me around the corner from the bus stop and then

"Hi!" and she dug one nail into the palm of my hand so that everything changed in a second.

Meanwhile the boss continued his attack, this time in a muted voice .

"She brought it to me there, even. You're sure you don't know anything about Anička? Tom, don't claim you don't know. Everybody knows about it. In Počernice and round about. And Božka showed me the letter just at the right moment at Strahov. It's a stupid business, Tom. You can't make money at it without some cheating."

Tom raised his glass and this time drank it down. Better keep his thoughts to himself. He only thought: Let's see what he'll do.

"Once only I drove her, Anička, from our place to Hloubětín, are you listening, Tom?" the boss said. "How far is that—two minutes? . . . Hey, Tom, and that was it. At midmorning she drove to the gardener's in Svépravice. You remember, the one who was cut down all of a sudden that time while he was installing electric heating in his greenhouse? They say he was going around barefoot and the damp soil under his feet was enough—he happened to touch the iron frame of the greenhouse. What the hell, I can't think what his name was."

The boss wiped his forehead and then, absentmindedly, poured for Tom and himself. The old lioness stretched out her hand as if she were dreamily recollecting some ancient trick that had succeeded in the enclosed circus ring, and on the rickety shelf she

switched on the radio. ". . . the march 'Hurray for
our Stakhanovites' by Ján Uhlíř," shouted the late-
model prewar bakelite Telefunken. The lion-tamer
made a skillful gesture and cut the din short. The
woman was again scanning the newspapers. Without
looking up, she handed a pack of Dukels to a young
man who with a clatter had come in from the street;
purely by touch she verified the money payment
while he sought to close the door behind himself as
quietly as possible. This allowed a bit of fresh air to
enter the former hut, and Tom gasped to breathe it
in with his lips and throat.

He needed that . . . So it was Anička vs. Božka, an
unequal contest. Just like my case. For the Sarolea I
won't make more than fifteen thousand, even if it's
polished down to the finest screw and it accelerates
from standing to one hundred in seven seconds.
And how much did the Jap cost? The boss had
never betrayed the secret. He'd bought it that time
right after his wedding to Božka—pardon—to Mrs.
Božka.

"Damn it, can't you remember," the boss continued. "As if to spite me he was half a head taller, but
gentle, kind, for today's times an improbable gardener
or businessman. And his father, some important
preacher, God only knows of what denomination, had
died around two years after him. He too was buried in
our place. They've got a small, narrow family grave,
almost in the middle, but a bit aside toward the railroad track. At least they can watch and see if the

12:05, the Baltic, or the other express is coming through, as the timetable has it. Remember when there was the other funeral? Members flocked to us from all over Bohemia and Moravia, just because, among those thousands who came to be smothered at the cemetery, there also came that former cabinet-member, the one with the moustache—what was his name? But they say he behaved himself and let all that treasonable rioting go without comment. He may have been a little bit scared they might bury him in the same grave as the preacher. Does anybody know what goes on in ministers' minds? Already as a young man before the war he put up, with his own hands, a twenty-meter chimney. That's when I was going to Sláma's in Mochov at five in the morning; I was their apprentice. And he, the gardener, already owned a Chevy and was raking it in for chimneys, greenhouses, and for his five or seven kids so that even before 4:00 a.m. he was riding that American machine to Prague to go to market so he'd get there first with his fresh lettuce. Was he on the black market with that? I don't think so. You wouldn't find him at the tavern, he didn't smoke, and seven or eight children plus his wife do eat up food. He toiled till his end, the preacher's second born. The first born had escaped in time to America rather than have to endure that sort of moral blackmail. That was what he called it, they say, in the Počernice elementary school, to which he walked from Svépravice. And there she was, Anička, in that postfuneral truck farm, before she appeared at the right side of the road as they approached Prague coming from Počernice, loaded down with one and a half satchels, when I went to Prague to order parts and borrowed the cycle that the chief of the Obuna chain kept at our place—you know him—Pánek."

He turned away from the checkered tablecloth and broke two matches before Tom reached for the box in his hand and managed to light the half-crumbled Lípa for him.

"You'd be a swell guy, Tom, if you'd just give up believing some things and start to get properly suspicious of some others. What should I tell you? I took Anička's satchel between my arms on my lap, and we were off. She laughed a little bit and said she'd never sat on a cycle before. So she held on to me tight from in back. Damn it, Tom. Was it going to happen? Or wasn't it? It happened. Last year in early May. They'd just sent her father back from the hospital with cancer; they couldn't do anything for him. He wasn't even fifty yet. They were so kind they gave him six hundred fifty-six crowns in pension, plus subsistence. She kept a half-time job typing at Czechoslovak Transport, and she took care of him and fed him. Her mother and brother had long since been knocked off during the last bombardment of the last of all conceivable wars. What a family! The bomb dropped the second day after they moved into a more or less new development—streetcar No. 19 goes there now—because the old man worked in Kolbenka. As a little girl Anička remembered how the Americans and British aimed on purpose at those collaborators of the Reich, so eager to get shoes and cigarettes. And eager for apartments, I shouldn't forget to say. The hard-working father and his half-orphaned daughter got as their reward half of a family cottage on the hill in Hloubětín. And that's where I drove. Her dad was still among the living then. His breathing was heavy, you could hear him through closed doors. No, I didn't go there right away. It was the third time when it happened. Her dad didn't want to go anywhere anymore; she had to give up her part-time job and stay with him. You must have seen her, Tom, don't tell me you didn't. In winter she worked a while at The Růžek until I had to haul her back to her dad, and we went dancing twice—because Božka was living with Uncle Michl in Brod: The salesgirl in his deli took maternity leave and he wouldn't have anybody else in the job."

At the bar there now stood a slight example of select Libeň elegance, a man in a brown jacket with red tie and neatly pressed beige trousers. Under the close-cropped skull there gathered an expression of suspense: When will I elicit their admiration? The hut was at that moment not precisely a suitable spot for such a purpose. So he went over toward the cardplayers and tried to present himself in a different form.

"Why, you've got no choice but to play that eight of hearts."

The cardplayers remained unfeeling and untouched, and so in self-defense he spoke to Tom and the boss.

"You tell them. The eight of hearts."

But even that pair were not struck favorably by him.

"Here you are, Mr. Vrbata," said the lion-tamer Kunst, and handed him a glass jug with a gilded rim, holding a liter.

With the squeaking of the door the Vrbata affair was over and Tom felt only the weight of the boss, Anička and Božka around his neck—and perhaps a bit farther in the distance, Jenka. Only *she* was no weight! The others were, of course. Cancer and the boss and Anička to boot. Jenka, I beg you, go to bed. I'm sure there's a lot of talk about the people in the village and elsewhere. Don't believe them. So she's called Anička. And the affair had really happened—when did he actually get married to Božka? Two years ago in the fall. Just before the Jap.

"Now I know . . . that reddish blonde," Tom said aloud.

"So you see—and try hard to remember," the boss raised his voice as if in self-defense or self-pity. "And it went on. Especially when her father really did die, and they told her at the town committee that her apartment was too big now and she'd have to make other plans. She worked it out this way: I was to get a divorce and move in with her as a lodger and so save the apartment. It was a special case, Tom. Even the bossiest Lutheran girls can be charming creatures on the surface. Only I'd had enough of it by then. And just because she'd recognized that, that beautiful, sweet, tender, unbearable Anička, the day before yesterday she wrote me a letter to tell me that life didn't exist for her without me. Can you imagine, Tom, that without me life for you—"

"Boss, let's leave that part out," Tom raised his head soberly, "Life is yours, life is Anička's, life is Mrs. Božka's or mine, and you can never know what anybody's life is worth."

"Except, Tom," the boss reached for his forearm, "women write to men only when you've had your fill of them. Why otherwise would they write, when they could come straight out and say it? So Anička wrote me day before yesterday that I'm the dearest and only guy and without me she doesn't want to go on in this world. More or less like that. And Božka the seamstress, of course, had nothing better to do than mend my jacket, because she supposed I'd be wearing it tonight at the Autoclub to go up on the podium and receive at least my honest due. Bullshit, Tom. She reached in the pocket and found that letter there. But what business did she have reaching into the pocket? Would you stand for that? It's true the sleeve was torn. But she could be excused for that—though it's also true that she had brought only enough dowry to pay for that Jap. Well, I'm going to sell it, Tom. Then I'll throw it under her feet—I'll trip her up the way she did me."

With his hands Tom straightened out the tablecloth, which the boss was rubbing nervously. Like him I won't make enough money for it, he thought with a shiver. Počernice had done enough gossiping about that. And I used to admire him because he had enough money for it himself. She sold the house, or he sold it, Božka's fellow, right away after the wedding. She got it from her parents, with a little shop out front and a yard in back, right off the Poděbrady highway. In normal times, half a million. Only when and where have we got normal times? One way or another the Czech Brethren bought it for a decent sum. Then they could still come up with the money when they wanted to. No, I wouldn't treat Jenka that way, even if she had anything worth stealing, but she's got nothing, right, Jenka, Jenička, thanks to fate!

"Tom, fellow, she found it there," the boss said. "What do you know about life? And she came there today with it, right there today, right after the first race. Even that one I didn't manage right, and after that it only got worse. Every time I ended up out-side, through my stupidity, as far out as the barrier. I couldn't even make a turn or throw it into a skid. And then Božka came up to the station and said, pale all over, "Josef, you're a yellow-livered chick-en—if you'd only try to come in first, second, third —but you're chicken." She threw Anička's letter at my feet, almost turned to go, so that I tried to pick it up, but she changed her mind and said: "That's just what you'd want!" She tore the letter out of my hand and was gone. So ride, racing-man.

With half-closed eyes Tom gazed at his boss. And I supposed all that time that it was the machine, he thought. That the Jap isn't really the best model. But it was Božka. She told him what he was. Anička, poor Anička.

"We're paid up, Boss, we can go." He straightened up stiffly and he felt a strong desire to wash himself, to wash himself all over.

The bottle of slivovitz was still half full. But Tom did not mind. He was ready to leave. The boss seized him by the shoulder with a firm hand and sat him down. The cardplayers looked around lazily and again back at their cards. You could hear only the rustling of the poster as the air stirred with the quick movement of the boss. The smoldering lioness trudged off to the door and only then glanced back at the lion-tamer.

"I'm going to bed. Don't forget to lock up the drawer, D'Artagnan. My feet are hurting me. The weather's changing."

Life's hard, lady, Tom thought to himself, but I won't give in as long as I've got Jenka. He pulled himself together, got up and looked straight into the boss's eyes. He saw that reddened face and told himself that he sure wouldn't want to have that Jap now. Another one. A yellow-livered chicken, she had called him. And he, Tom, had always thought that the boss would let himself go and lean the way you have to lean when you take a curve. You could do it with a Jap like that. But *he* certainly never would. Even now he wouldn't permit himself a second ride on it. He wouldn't dare.

That shouldn't be counted among his worst sins, Tom's father the upholsterer might well have said.

The boss slowly leaned his back against the wall, began to button his expensive leather vest, and reached for the checkered cap from the coat hook.